Cult Keeper

Melanie Miller Hollis

ISBN-13:   978-0692625002

ISBN-10:   0692625003

Chapter 1

"I think we need to observe her for a few days and plan to go back in to do a second surgery next week," said the stoic cardiologist in the white coat whose name tag bore only one name: Ammi. "My concern is the aneurysm. I don't want to frighten you, but if it were to erupt, it could mean sudden death."

Sudden death. The two words, spoken almost too nonchalantly by the beautiful Israeli, hung precariously in the air. Mary noted the doctor's name tag again as her mind darted, randomly seeking others who were known by a single name: Oprah, Cher, Sting, Dolly…"God, Mare," she thought, yanking herself back into the present, "your daughter may die a sudden death and all you can think about is a bunch of random celebrities?"

The time in the hospital had been beyond difficult. Night after night trying to sleep on a recliner that was supposedly engineered to turn into a makeshift bed had left her feeling more zombie than human. She had asked around and had not found a single person who had slept well in those "comfortable" recliners. Turning toward the other person who had just walked in the door, Mary hoped to hear a more encouraging opinion than Ammi's. He spoke before she had a chance to collect her thoughts.

"It's up to you, Mary," he offered while washing his hands in the nearby sink. "If you line up nine other cardiologists in this room alongside me, we will not all agree on this case. However, you need to know that I respectfully disagree with Dr. Ammi."

The cardiologist who had cared for Miss Charity since she was in her momma's womb gave a polite nod toward his younger female counterpart while rubbing his hands together to warm them; he sounded sure of himself. "The surgeon couldn't locate the aneurysm in Miss Charity's heart during the procedure when her heart was stopped, so I don't believe any more surgery will change that fact. In my opinion, another surgery this soon, especially one considered exploratory, would present too much risk for our girl."

Pausing only for a moment, possibly to allow his words to settle in and take hold, Mary watched as he took a few long strides across the floor to reach the little angel whose exposed chest looked too much like a mangled railroad track. Miss Charity had many strikes against her, according to her mother, more than any human deserved. In addition to the complicated heart issues, she was born with an extra chromosome and remained non-verbal. Mary, a courageous warrior, often questioned how long she would have to fight the tide of the world for the sake of her daughter who lay sleeping, oblivious to the conversation.

The kind doctor, placing his hand on Miss Charity's head, whispered: "Why don't we give this some time, Mary? Take the little cheese puff home, let her heal, and then bring her back in six months for an echocardiogram. If things have taken a turn at that time, we may need to have another discussion about more surgery. But let's not get the proverbial cart before the horse, all right?"

Mary's eyes nervously darted between the two as she wondered why two professionals, sharing the same field of expertise, couldn't agree on treatment. Why weren't GiGi and Poppy there with her? Worried about Tate and Wills, they had insisted on rushing back to Mary's house to make sure both had eaten, and the timing was horrible. Because she needed them there. With her. Now.

"As you know, Dr. King," she muttered, feeling like a freak show, "my personal life is sort of a mess, which means I am not thinking very clearly. Are you saying I can take my baby girl home?"

"Yes, that's what I'm saying." His voice was reassuring, positive, firm, and upbeat.

Ammi broke in abruptly. "And yet I disagree."

Mary pretended not to hear the retort; instead, she quickly confided in the one she trusted: "I want to go home. Good Lord, you cannot imagine how badly I want to go home! We have been in this hospital for more than three weeks now, and I'm so sick of this place."

Vulnerable and tired, Mary's voice began to break. She sat down on the chair beside Miss Charity's hospital bed, opposite Dr. King, and laid her head on the cool white sheets partially covering the little one resting beneath them. "And I know this one with the battle wounds wants to go home, too."

Dr. King, back in business mode, retrieved the stethoscope hanging precariously around his neck and rubbed it on his hand to warm it. Mary watched him closely as he carefully listened to the exposed chest. Seeming somewhat satisfied with what he'd heard, he sighed out loud: "Then go home, Mary. Take your baby girl home. It really is that simple. Just go home."

"But what if…" Mary's eyes grew wide, full of fear.

Dr. Ammi, ready to pounce on any sign of weakness, interjected: "The 'what-if' is what I'm most concerned about, Mrs. Montgomery."

"No need to think about what-ifs," Dr. King returned without hesitation. "Right now we can only work with what we know. We know Miss Charity has an aneurysm in her heart. We know it appears to be stable. We know the surgeon tried to locate it during the open-heart surgery while Miss Charity's heart was stopped but couldn't find it. And if he couldn't find it three weeks ago, why do you think he would be able to find it now?"

With that pointed question, which somehow made perfect sense to a very weary momma, the matter was settled. Dr. King brought the discharge papers into the room, and within two hours, Mary was on the way home with her heart patient.

Seven months had passed since Philip left his family. Seven months. The Bible was full of sevens, and the irony that Charity's heart would stop on the day that marked those long seven months was not lost on Mary. Even though her husband's affair with Bonnie only lasted a few paltry weeks, the guilt wouldn't allow him to return to Mary. The divorce would be final soon. He was giving his soon-to-be ex-wife everything she asked for; he hadn't risen up to fight her on a single issue.

As Mary drove down the interstate, carrying Miss Charity back toward home, thoughts of seeing Philip in the hospital drove her nuts. Why had she wanted to comfort him when she saw him crying in the waiting room during the three-hour surgery? And confide in him when the medical staff riddled her with questions? She hated him; that much she knew. But there was still that hole inside her heart that—

Her cell phone rang midthought. "Hey, Mom. I've got the baby girl snuggled tight in her car seat, and she can't wait to see you guys." Mary spoke with the most chipper, carefree voice she could muster. She was quite the actress.

GiGi had faithfully held the rest of the family together during her daughter's absence. While she was excited for Miss Charity and Mary to return home, she was even more excited to go back to her home and sleep in her own bed. She had faithfully traveled back and forth to the hospital every day, homeschooled Tate, cooked, and cleaned. More than anything else, however, she had become the rock for her daughter and grandkids to lean on. The woman who was now affectionately known by her family for having more grit and tenacity than an old hungry hound stalking a family reunion cookout felt flat as a flitter. When she learned that the hospital was releasing Miss Charity, exhaustion had settled in and taken over. The woman was beat.

"Listen, Mare Bear, your dad and I think it would be best if we went on home before you get here," she suggested. "We don't want to steal any thunder from Tater Bug and Wills, you know? They are so excited for you two to get back here. If we stayed, we'd probably just be a big old distraction."

She took a deep breath, hoping Mary would take the bait.

"Mom, you have done so much to help out. I really want you to be there to welcome Miss Charity home. You do want to see us, don't you?"

"Oh goodness, I'm walking out the door. Your dad's already in the car and it's running." The wise fox quickly changed the subject. "I cooked dinner for you guys, one of your favorite meals. It's warmed up and waiting on you in the oven, honey. I'm sure you'd just gag if you had to eat one more hospital meal, wouldn't you?"

"Really? Are you sure you have to leave?" Mary's gentle voice revealed sincere disappointment.

"Well, you know your daddy. Once he sets his mind to something, he is tough to budge. Hold on a second. I'm climbing in the car right now."

"Mom?"

"Yes, I can still hear you. You're on the speaker now. The Bluetooth picked up the call, so say hello to Pops."

"Daddy?" That single word broke the floodgates, and tears started to flow down both of Mary's cheeks. She had always been a daddy's girl.

He answered her as if nothing at all were wrong in the world, as if he couldn't hear her crying, "Yep, it's me."

"I'm scared, Daddy."

"What are you scared of, sugar?" He knew. In fact, he probably knew Mary better than she knew herself, but he asked the question anyway. She needed to talk, and he was ready to listen.

Pushing back the desire to break down completely, Mary gulped back a gigantic heap of sorrow. "What if her heart stops again?"

"Then you call nine-one-one again, just like you did before."

"But what if this time it stops when I'm asleep? And I can't save her?"

There it was. Mary had been petrified to speak her fear out loud, but now, on the way home with Miss Charity, she had no choice but to face it. GiGi reached over and clinched her husband's bicep hard. He reached up, putting his index finger to his lips, motioning for her to remain silent.

"That's a possibility. It could happen." His voice was still steady and calm. It nearly broke his heart to say it, but he knew Mary had to hear the hard truth if she was ever going to win the battle. Coddling her by watering it all down wouldn't help at all.

"I can't do this, Pops. Please go back to the house and stay with me tonight. I just need help getting through this first night," Mary pleaded. "I know I've asked a lot from you all, but if you'd just give me one more night…"

"Nope, we're not going to be able to do that, Mary." GiGi and Poppy could hear the sobs through the car's speakers as they drove through Cleveland, Tennessee. It was becoming nearly impossible for them to hold their resolve. But tough love won out. "You are stronger than you think you are," her dad continued, "and you have to keep hanging on to Jesus. We're all hanging on to Him together through all of this, right?"

"Please stay?" It was all she could manage.
"No, Mary."

She clicked to end the call, hanging up on her parents, and slammed the steering wheel with both hands, screaming as loud as her voice would allow. "I hate You, God!" she bawled. "I hate You, and I hate my life!"

Chapter 2

A few days passed before Mary heard from either her parents or Philip. Ironically, they called to check in on the same day. Still feeling overwhelmed, she gave both phone calls the best Southern snub she could muster. As for Tate, she was elated to have her momma and little sister back home. And Wills, for some reason, had been relentlessly needling his mom about his new girlfriend, wanting to invite her over for dinner so Mary could meet her.

"You'll love her," he said.

"I'm sure I'll love her, but please give me a few days to catch up with the real world before you bring a new friend over."

"But her whole family has been praying for Miss Charity nonstop." His voice was laced with urgency; this girl meant something to him. "Emma can't wait to meet my li'l sis…and you," he spoke with the typical hysteria accompanying young love. "Plus," he added, "she is much more than just a new friend to me."

"Nonstop prayer, huh?" Mary was folding laundry, barely paying attention, but trying to appease her son. "Forgive me, but I doubt that."

"What?" Wills asked, trying to figure out where his mother was coming from. He honestly believed she would be thrilled to know that Emma and her family had been praying for his little sister, so her disinterest threw him.

"You said she and her family prayed for Miss Charity nonstop, which I find difficult to believe. In case you haven't noticed the obvious, their saintly prayers weren't answered." Mary was being curt with her son and knew it. "If their prayers had been answered, and if my baby girl no longer had a serious heart issue, I would be overjoyed to have your new friend and her family over to thank them for their prayers." Throwing the folded towels into the basket rather sharply, Mary stood, picked up the basket, and set her jaw. "But since Little Miss is not healed, it is not going to happen, at least not any time soon."

"Mom, please focus on me instead of Miss Charity for just a minute," Wills pleaded, hoping to get through to his mom but still treading lightly. "I don't think you realize it, but you haven't been normal lately."

Mary, not appreciating any free counsel offered from her teenage son, paused, shifted the laundry basket to one hip, and gave him an angry glare. "Normal? I know you did not just throw that word at me." Her eyes bore into him; she didn't even blink. "Wow, Wills, I am so happy to hear that all you want is a big dose of normal. Why didn't I think of that?"

The teenage boy immediately felt like he was a six-year-old again and sincerely wished he could retract the comment. A sermon was coming.

"How can I possibly be normal when my life has fallen apart?" Mary continued, preaching in a high-pitched tone that rang like a siren throughout the house. "You do remember that your father ran off to have a fling with your best friend's mother, right?"

"Ex-best friend," Wills broke in.

"Yeah, about that," Mary quipped, "how is it that Crew's crazy mom and her out-of-control hormones have become his fault? I don't blame him, so why do you?"

"I don't want to talk about it."

"You never want to talk about it, yet I'm the one who's not normal? Maybe you need to consider taking a psychology class or two when you go to college, Wills, because I'm pretty sure you would be considered 'Not Normal 101' right along with me!"

Mary finally took a breath, so her son took the opportunity and ran with it. "Let's don't fight, Mom, please. I know you're stressed and worried about Miss Charity, and I really don't mean to cause you any more stress." His voice oozed with humility. "I just wanted you to meet Emma, that's all. She and her family have helped me so much while you've been gone."

Wills wiped a tear from his eye before it could fall; he didn't want her to see. But Mary did see. And she softened. Her son's puppy-dog eyes had always melted her. For an instant, she wondered why she allowed herself to take all the bottled-up rage out on him. She'd been doing that too often, and he didn't deserve it. Tossing the laundry basket on the floor, Mary reached out for Wills's hand and pulled him close. He stood so tall above her, tall enough that she rested her head on his shoulder and did what she knew she would end up doing all along.

"All right, you big lug," she said, sighing, "invite Emma to come over tomorrow night for dinner and tell her to bring her whole family with her."

"All of them?"

"Yes," she said, ashamed of the way she had acted, "I might as well knock the Duggars out all at once, right?"

Wills pulled his momma in tight to him and kissed her on the head. "Not funny, but thanks, Mom."

Pushing the Pause button on her anxiety, Mary breathed in the moment as her son held her. She smelled the familiar Polo cologne mixed with the Doritos he had been caught munching on in the kitchen, and she considered how fast time had passed them by. She wished she could make it stand still but knew this moment, too, would soon be a distant memory. "I'm sorry for fussing at you," she added as he pulled away.

Wills, happy to have his mother connect with him again, gave her a big smile, pronouncing the dimple in his left cheek. "Do you remember that brownie GiGi was supposed to bring to you at the hospital a couple of weeks ago? And when you opened the box, it was empty?" he asked, giggling.

Mary, clearly seeing where this was going, answered slyly, "Why, yes, Wills, yes I do. As I recall, GiGi blamed the bakery for forgetting to put my brownie in the box, but now I'm supposing there is a different answer to that problem."

Sensing his mom was willing to play, Wills tore off through the house in a mad dash, and Mary, forgetting her troubles, ran after him, in a full sprint, hurling laundry at him as she ran. "How could you eat my brownie?" she screamed. "You are a thief, Wills Montgomery!"

The two laughed as they played their silly game. Mary needed that silly game. Finally, feeling exhausted, she plopped back on the couch and gave up. "I surrender."

"Let's just call it even," Wills heckled. "You fussed at little old innocent me, and I didn't deserve it—" he began.

"And you ate my brownie." Mary, still out of breath, completed his thought. "My fudge-covered, scrumptious, chewy brownie."

"And I loved every bite of it," Wills said, not quite ready to end the ribbing.

Mary picked up a hand towel and, mustering the little bit of strength she had left, tossed it in his direction. "Alrighty then, I take back my apology for fussing at you earlier," she said, "because you had it coming to you, didn't you?"

Wills grabbed the towel out of the air, rolled it into a ball, and threw it right back at his momma, popping her on the head. "Wills Montgomery!" she yelled, as he ran off laughing hysterically.

As soon as he was out of earshot, Mary swallowed her pride and called her mom to inform her about the big dinner plans.

"I'm still mad at you and dad, but I need some help," she began.

GiGi couldn't help herself. She pranced her petite high-heeled feet all around her tiled kitchen floor and squeaked, "Finally! Thank the Lord you haven't forsaken your parents!"

"Oh, I am still forsaking you," Mary responded gruffly, picturing GiGi doing a happy jig as she listened to the high heels clicking, "I'm probably going to be forsaking you for a long time for leaving me in charge in this house all on my own."

This was what GiGi called make or break time. She knew what she chose to say next would either further distance her daughter or reel her back in. So she paused, took a breath, and pulled back the curtain a little bit so Mary could see.

"Listen, baby girl, the last thing on earth your daddy and I wanted to do was leave you in charge in that house on your own. Every fiber of our being wanted to stay there and be in charge ourselves, taking care of you and Miss Charity."

"I don't understand," Mary responded. "Then why did you leave?"

"Lord, we had to leave and let you stand on your own two feet. That's the toughest job a parent has to do. You'll find that out soon enough when Wills goes off to college."

"You really wanted to stay?"

"More than anything in the world. We haven't slept a wink since we left your house, and that's the God's honest truth. We drive by your house a dozen times a day, just hoping to get a glimpse of one of you through the front windows so we'll know everybody is doing OK. Literally, we are dying over here."

And with that, GiGi was back in. Why is it that misery always loves company? It dawned upon Mary, after realizing the truth behind her father's momentary madness, that her parents were every bit as tormented as she was. And that made her strangely happy. Nearly giddy, in fact.

"Oh good. I mean…I'm sorry, Momma."

"Well, I'm sorry, too. But let's put that behind us and move on to whatever it is you need me to help you with."

"I'm hosting a dinner party tomorrow night for Emma's whole family. Mister Young, Tall, Irresistible, and Handsome guilted me into it."

"The whole family?" GiGi asked with a smirk, knowing her daughter had never had an easy time saying no to Wills about anything.

"Yep," Mary snapped back, still unsure whether they could pull it off. "That's the plan."

"You do know how many are in that family, don't you?" GiGi cackled, considering the mountain of work that would have to be done.

Emma and Wills had met at a contemporary Christian concert in Chattanooga while Miss Charity was in the hospital, and the two had been inseparable ever since. Number one in what had become a long line of nine children, Emma had spent a lot of time over at the Montgomery house with Wills during Mary's absence. It was no big surprise that GiGi had become very fond of the teenage beauty during her charge. Emma, homeschooled herself, had jumped in with both feet to help the larger-than-life grandma cook, clean, and teach Tate. So she was excited to hear the news of the long-awaited introduction and especially looked forward to meeting the rest of Emma's family.

"I have an idea that you will find either brilliant or batty," she proclaimed to Mary with a sly grin evident in her voice.

"Want to hear it?"

Chapter 3

The evening of the big dinner party couldn't have been more perfect. The weather was mild with just a smidgen of bitter cold, while the glow of a full moon lit up the old house on Ocoee Street, inviting the guests to enter, find warmth, and have a good time. Thanksgiving had rudely passed Mary's family without even a slight nod this year. The youngest Montgomery was released from the hospital only a few short days following the annual holiday, so GiGi, ready to right the wrong, had worked sixteen hours straight to help Mary pull off a Thanksgiving feast rivaling the one at Plymouth Rock for Emma's family as well as her own.

Even Mary's sister, Viv, had taken a sick day from work to be in charge of the decor. And she spared no expense. Pumpkins in every color, shape, and size adorned each corner and tabletop while burlap cloth teeming with fancy orange-and-gold ribbon meandered about freely, punctuating the fall occasion. No detail was overlooked, right down to the homemade pinecone place-card holders that had been carefully crafted to mimic turkeys, propping up the name of each one who would attend the almost impromptu event.

"Had *Southern Living* magazine editors been told about this occasion in time, they surely would have given it a prime spot in the harvest edition," Mary remarked, hugging Viv. "You've outdone yourself; it really is that fantastic!"

GiGi was still busy in the kitchen. "All right, I've put out the glazed ham, candied yams, green bean casserole, fried okra, creamed corn, and the yeast rolls," she spoke as she checked off her list. "Have I forgotten anything?"

"Well if you have," Viv answered, "it's too late now. Emma's family is pulling into the driveway right now."

Wills bounded to the front door with Mary in tow, absentmindedly flinging the door wide open. The door handle banged into the foyer's wall, creating a startling gong sound, which he utilized to initiate his big announcement: "Welcome to our belated Thanksgiving feast," his voice rang out. "Welcome, welcome, welcome!"

Mary instinctively shot her son a quick sideways glance. "Goodness, when did you become such a corn ball?" she teased, standing at the door beside him while Emma's family began unloading from a white, sixteen-passenger van. Not getting much of a reaction, she then poked him in the ribs and mocked him with her best imitation of Gomer Pyle: "Welcome, welcome, welcome." Mary expected a big laugh, but instead, Wills completely ignored her. In fact, it was quite possible he never heard her, because without giving a hint of notice, he rushed down the front steps, taking on the sidewalk with gazelle-like strides. Within seconds, he was out at the van helping unload the masses.

Viv, by this time, was standing next to her sister with hands planted firmly on her hips, not holding back her skepticism toward what she considered to be an outrageously large family. Both squinted their eyes to better take in the unfolding scene. Car seats were unlatched, children climbed out, yet there was no chaos. The quiet order unnerved Viv.

"I deal with kids every day at work," she whispered, "and trust me, those aren't normal kids."

Within moments, all nine children marched down the sidewalk in a single file line toward the sisters. One of the youngest children was propped on top of Wills's shoulders as they forged forward. Emma's parents followed behind them all. With one hand, her mother casually held a young child on her hip while holding her husband's hand with the other. Smiles beamed from their faces.

Wills made introductions at the door. Each child eagerly shook both Mary's and Viv's hands, thanking them for the dinner invitation. Emma was the last child to enter and was just ahead of her parents. She threw her arms around Mary's neck: "Mrs. Montgomery, I am so happy to finally meet you! Welcome back home!"

"Well, I'm happy to meet you, too, sweetie," Mary responded, taken a wee bit off guard by Emma's overwhelming warmth. "Here, meet my sister, Viv." Mary pulled her sister close. "Unlike you, I didn't come from a very big family," Mary gushed. "It's just the two of us, right, Viv?"

"Thank goodness it was just the two of you!" GiGi called

out from the other room. "Now let Emma go so she can come in here and give the one who loves her a big old hug."

The teen girl with long brown curls giggled just before skipping out of the foyer and into the kitchen to greet GiGi. Within five minutes, the two families were standing hand-in-hand in a circle, prepared to give thanks to the Lord for the bounty of food His hand had provided.

"Brian, since Philip is not here this evening, would you do the honors?" GiGi suggested.

And Brian, Emma's father, was more than happy to oblige. "Yeshua," he began, "you have brought us together this evening and we are truly grateful. For this feast that has been prepared and for the ones who prepared it all, we give you thanks. We ask you to bless it and use it to give us strength so we may serve You more. Amen."

GiGi demanded, in the nicest way possible, that Emma's family fix their plates first. They were the guests, after all. The food was set up buffet style, so they all formed a line and began serving themselves. Mary excused herself and was checking on Miss Charity when Viv walked into the bedroom.

"How's Little Miss?" her sister asked.

"Right now the pain meds keep her sleeping most of the day," Mary said while gently brushing the hair off the sleeping beauty's face. She tucked the blankets tight around the snoozing little body and nuzzled her nose against her ear. "She looks like an angel when she sleeps," she whispered. "You'd never guess her chest looks like an old train track, would you?"

Viv took Mary's hand into her own and held it tight. "I love you, Mare." She didn't know what else to say.

Mary needed her family more than she'd ever needed them in her life.

She pulled her sister's hand up to her face and kissed the backside of it. "I love you, too, Sis."

"We better get back out to our company," Viv said, pivoting toward the bedroom door, "or else they may eat all the food without us. There are so many of them."

"By the way, do you know who Yeshua is?" Mary asked with a chuckle, following her.

"Who?"

"Yeshua," Mary repeated. "Did you not hear Brian's prayer? He prayed to Yeshua."

"No he did not." She paused. "Did he?"

"Yes! I nearly choked when he said it." Mary folded her arms and shook her head. "I wonder why he didn't pray to

Jesus?" she whispered. "I thought they were Christians."

Viv busted out in a big laugh, and before Mary had time to think about it, she was bent over, holding her sides, laughing, too. Neither of them knew why the subject struck them funny, but it did.

Mary, now laughing so hard she snorted when trying to breathe, managed: "Who is Yeshua, Viv? Is my son dating someone who is in a cult?"

"That would just about be your luck," Viv answered, giggling just as heartily as her sister, "truly, that would be your luck."

GiGi, growing concerned about the disappearance of her daughters, found them cackling away in Miss Charity's room. She tore into the room, instantly dampening the mood. "What in the good Lord's name are you two doing in here?" she asked. "You're acting like you did when you were teenagers. For once and for all, would y'all just grow up and then let it stick for a while?"

Viv and Mary straightened up, gathering their composure. Viv then answered: "Do you mean what in Yeshua's name are we doing in here?"

And with that, they both busted out in unrestrained laughter once again. GiGi was incredulous. "I can't believe you would make fun of our guests and our Lord at the same time. Have you both gone mad? Yeshua is the Jewish name for Jesus. Don't you girls know anything? Now get yourselves together and come take care of your guests!"

GiGi turned on her six-inch heels and prissed right out of the room, closing the door firmly behind her.

"Viv, we've got to go back out there. But you have to make a deal with me first, OK?"

Viv, still tickled, wiped tears of laughter from her eyes. "A deal? I think I can do that, especially if it has anything to do with figuring out what kind of religion your son's new girlfriend is practicing."

"Are you kidding me?" Mary became very serious. "The deal is that you cannot ask that man why he calls Jesus by the name Yeshua. Don't even mention religion or faith or anything like that. Please. Wills seems to like this girl, and I don't want to do anything to screw it up for him."

"What's in this deal for me?" Viv needled her sister, hoping to get a rise. "It better be good, because I want to know if Wills is dating a kooky cult follower more than I want to eat all that good food Mom has been slaving over. I really do."

The table was full when the sisters finally wandered back into the dining area. GiGi drilled the girls with an evil eye, but they both ignored it. "Viv and I were just looking in on Miss Charity," Mary explained, "and you'll all be happy to know she is resting peacefully." Grabbing her plate, she began at the front of the buffet line, "Wills tells me you all have been praying for her nonstop, so before you leave tonight, I'd like for you to feel free to go in and peek at her."

"Oh, thank you, Mary. We all want to see the little angel, and pray over her, too, but we'll be careful not to wake her. It is wonderful news that she is back home," Brian replied. "Our whole fellowship has been praying for her healing."

The subject was on the table. Viv hadn't opened the door. Brian had.

"Where do you go to, uhmmm, fellowship?" Viv didn't resist the opportunity. Both Viv and her sister were still gathering food from the buffet spread, looking down at those who were seated at the table eating. Mary, not caring at all if anyone noticed, reached across the spread of food and pinched her sister's arm hard. Viv got the message, but didn't give a hoot.

"We go to the Lost Tribe Fellowship." It was a subject that appeared to make Brian excited, because he answered with absolute glee. "Have you heard of it?"

"No, I can't say that I have heard of the Lost Tribe Fellowship," Viv replied, serving a heaping spoonful of candied yams onto her plate. "Why don't you tell us all about it?"

"It would probably be best if we invited you for a visit to

our fellowship," his wife, Diana, suggested. "All of you should attend service with us sometime. It's the most wonderful group of people we've ever known. They are all like family to us. You'd fit right in, and I believe you would love it!"

"That would be hard to do since we have our own church service on Sundays," Mary spoke up, hoping to put an end to the subject before Viv had a chance to dig into the matter any further and risk embarrassing them all. "But thank you for the invitation." She made her way to the table and began eating.

Brian quickly jumped back in. "Oh, we don't meet on Sundays. We meet on the Sabbath Day, just like Yeshua and His followers did."

Viv's face must have shown what she was feeling, which was sheer confusion. "Our church meets on the Sabbath Day, too, Brian, on Sunday."

"The true Sabbath Day is on Saturday," Brian explained, as if it was something every spiritual person should know. "You all are aware of that, I'm sure, right?"

Just as Brian was opening the floodgates about his thoughts on the Sabbath Day, GiGi was noticing that no one in Emma's family had taken a portion of her honey-glazed ham. Out of nowhere, she unexpectedly smacked the table with her open hand and shouted: "You all are Jewish! It makes perfect sense. You call Jesus by the Jewish name,

Yeshua, you make a big deal out of the Sabbath, and you don't eat pork!"

Everyone at the table turned to look at her. It was one of those moments when time stopped and stood still.

To break the awkward silence, GiGi decided she better save the day. "We don't have a problem with it, so don't worry. This family loves everybody…African American people, Muslims, Catholics, Asians, and even the Native Americans. We love them all!"

Since no one was jumping into the conversation with her, she kept forging on at breakneck speed. "Sometimes Poppy slips up and calls the natives of America the Indians, but I am always quick to remind him they like to be properly called the Native Americans. The word 'Indian' just sounds much too primitive, and I think they take it as a slam. It makes you think of those hideous scalpings when they would dance around a totem pole and yank the hair right off the head of a cowboy, you know. For me, it's a matter of being respectful. Jesus said to love all people, so we do." She kept rambling on and on, making her family as nervous as a cat on bath day. "Oh Lordy, I just used the name Jesus around a bunch of Jews, didn't I? A whole table full of Jews. I should've said that 'God' said to love all people, because to us Christians, God and Jesus are the same, but I know you Jews don't see it that way. I'm sorry. I'm just going to have to get used to being around God's chosen people, which, of course, is what you are. We certainly aren't. We're just a bunch of Gentiles who were saved by the blood of Jesus when you all rejected Him and murdered Him on the cross."

Viv couldn't take it anymore. "Mom!" she practically shouted. "Please, hush!"

"Yes, for the love of Pete, hush up!" repeated Poppy, equally as riled up.

Brian, in response, laughed out loud, which caused both families to turn their attention away from GiGi and toward him just as Diana lifted her shirt and began nursing the baby. There it was, her right breast, in plain view, for everyone to see.

"Glory!" GiGi sputtered, standing up from the table and raising her hands up high. "Cover that thing up! We can all see it!"

Brian began laughing louder. "It's natural," he said, looking down at the baby, "and beautiful. We believe it's what Yahweh intended when He created Adam and Eve."

"Not in front of my grandchildren and my husband, He didn't," she responded. "It's why He gave animal skins to Adam and Eve. The naked are supposed to be covered. It's in the Good Book. Now please, Diana, cover that thing up so we can all enjoy our Thanksgiving meal."

Brian wasn't about to let the old Granny of the group have her way without standing his ground. This time he spoke with only a slight smirk; the laughter had completely disappeared from his voice. "No, she is not going to cover up the most natural act the Creator gave a woman," he told her while making a face that implied the elder woman should know better. "When she uses her body to give nourishment, it is her way of celebrating Yahweh and how He nourishes and feeds us with His Word."

"Are you trying to rewrite God's Holy Word?" The old bird was fired up now. "There isn't a time in the whole Bible where God says women need to breast-feed at a table where people are trying to eat, and absolutely no correlation between breast-feeding and the Word of God. That's one of the nuttiest things I think I've ever heard, and it doesn't make a lick of sense. Not a lick."

GiGi's words were flying out of her mouth. The longer she stood, watching Diana breast-feeding the baby in full view, the faster she spouted off.

"I can hear that baby sucking, everybody can hear it, and now I've lost my appetite. All this good food…that I graciously made with my own hands…and I can't even eat a bite of it. And I've looked forward to eating it." Her arms were flailing about; she was in full lecture mode. "C'mon, Pops and Tater Bug, let's go check on Miss Charity while Diana finishes up the most natural act God has given her." After taking a few steps away from the table, GiGi turned and chimed back in. "And Wills, if I find out you've been looking anywhere in the general direction of that woman's breast, so help me, I will get a hickory stick from the backyard and beat your fanny really good when everybody leaves." She stomped away, Poppy and Tate behind her, stunned.

Once the noise died down…well, once GiGi stopped preaching…Viv decided to dig a bit deeper. "So you all are Jewish?" she asked, intentionally cutting a big piece of ham and popping it promptly into her mouth.

"No, we're not Jewish," replied Brian, acting as if the loaded question didn't bother him at all. "We're followers of Yeshua, the One you call Jesus, just like you."

Mary made a decision to turn her ears off. The whole nightmare scene with GiGi had already worn her out. Any discussion between Viv and Brian, each who appeared to be as hardheaded as the other, would probably not end well, either. She looked around the table, taking time to soak in the face of each child present. They all seemed happy and content, and why wouldn't they be? They had a mother and a father who loved each other. A home. Not a broken home. Mary felt the familiar stab of pain in her chest. The pain that always accompanied thoughts of the Chief. The one who had been her high school sweetheart. The only man she had ever loved. This had been the first Thanksgiving meal in more years than she cared to count that she'd spent without him. Wills caught her eye and gave her a pity grin. She hated the pity grin. He knew what she was thinking, because he was probably thinking the same thing. They weren't a family anymore.

"…and if you follow the commands of Yahweh, which most Christians don't, you will be free from sickness, from heartache, and from sin."

Brian's words broke Mary from her thoughts.

"What did you just say?" Mary asked, butting into the conversation.

"I was saying that my family has found the secret that has been hidden in the scriptures for the faithful to find. The way to avoid sickness, heartache, and sin. We've been practicing our faith this way for many years now, and haven't had any sickness in our family. With nine children, and another on the way in about seven months, I'd say there is something to it, wouldn't you?" He seemed confident, yet not arrogant. He believed he held some answers Mary was seeking. And then he went a step further. "Mary, we are aware that your marriage is quite possibly ending, and we are so sorry about that." His voice was sincere; he meant every word.

"I guarantee if you and Philip had followed the scriptures as Diana and I have, your marriage would not only be strong today, but would be vibrant, just as ours is." He bent over and kissed Diana on the cheek. "Most important, though, Miss Charity's heart would be healed."

Mary's mouth dropped open. Was this it? Could it be? Was God using this family to show her the way for her daughter to be healed? For her marriage to be saved? Her heart began to beat violently as the tips of her fingers tingled.

Viv, concerned about her sister, interrupted. "God has already healed Miss Charity. She made it through surgery against the odds and is still very alive."

"Alive," Brian countered, "but not healed. And the Father very much wants to give her a brand-new heart, but He is waiting on Mary and Philip's faith and obedience." He paused and looked right into Mary's eyes. "That is a word He gave me for you this evening, Mary. This must begin with you. That is why we are here. This meal was preordained by the Father for you."

By this time, Diana had finished nursing the baby who was now fast asleep in her arms. The old bird chirped from the nearby room: "Yoo-hoo…is everything covered up? Has Diana stopped nourishing her baby?"

"Yes, Momma, please come on back in here now," Viv said. "I think you and Pops are going to want to be in on this conversation."

But Brian was finished talking. He referred to a verse about casting your pearls before swine and refused to speak any more about his faith. As a matter of fact, he told them all if they wanted to know more, they needed to visit his fellowship. Mary intended to do just that.

Chapter 4

Philip was at work when the phone call came in, and within minutes he had told his office assistant he planned to take the remainder of the day off. Jenkins Deli may have only been a short drive from his office, but he was sweating bullets about the lunch meeting by the time he arrived. The caller was someone Philip had heard of but had never met, and when the man mentioned he had information about Mary, Philip immediately became antsy. More than curiosity urged him to find out what this man knew about his wife. The divorce was well on its way, but until the judge signed the paperwork, erasing the marriage, Philip held on with white knuckles to the dream of putting his family back together. Maybe this lunch meeting would be a step in that direction.

Introductions were made rather informally as the three settled into a corner booth in the bar area. Humming with the midday business crowd, a toy train chugged along a track over their heads, announcing a local's birthday in red digital lights, while classic rock radio exploded through the speakers. An expected one- or two-hour lunch meeting turned into nearly five hours; they each drank buckets of the sweetest freshly brewed tea in town as time passed quickly.

After Philip pulled into his driveway, feeling electrified by renewed hope, he turned the ignition and pulled out his keys. Leaning his head on the steering wheel, he began to pray out loud: "Lord, you know my heart. I don't deserve to ask you for help, so I won't. But please, before I take the steps I am beginning to take to save my marriage, forgive me."

He dropped his keys and cell phone onto the kitchen table, and for the first time, noticed a missed call from Preacher Walker. The man had left a short message asking Philip to return the call, but Philip didn't. As a matter of fact, it would be a long time before the elder pastor, the one who had become Philip's most trusted confidant, would hear from him. If Philip was going to make his family believe, he had to make everyone else believe, too.

The game plan was on!

Brian Dilbeck called Mary, inviting her to their Sabbath service, and she couldn't resist. "Bring the whole family," he had said, "even Miss Charity. If she needs to lie down in your lap through the entire service, that won't be a problem. We want her there so we can pray over her." That excited Mary. She invited Poppy, GiGi, and Viv to come along, too. They all met at Mary's house on the fellowship's Sabbath Day, which was Saturday, and then she and the kids followed her parents and Viv over to the plaza where the religious service would take place. A portable sign with a big flashing arrow pointed them to the place of worship. Poppy pulled into a space marked for visitors, and Mary pulled in right beside him. Rolling down her window, GiGi leaned over and motioned for Mary to let her window down: "Honey, did you read that flashing sign? Did you see what it said?"

Mary couldn't quite make out Viv in the back seat; her father's windows were too dark, but it looked like she was either laughing or crying.

"Is Viv all right?" Mary asked.

GiGi glanced back at Viv, who was now lying down in the seat. "She's as crazy as a loon, and if she doesn't calm down, I'm going to whack her with my purse," she huffed, with an intentional sharp tone. "But, honey, back to my question…" Her tone switched on a dime, now becoming smooth as butter. "Did you read that flashing sign out front?"

"No I didn't, but what is wrong with Viv? Is she laughing or crying?"

"Both," Pops chimed in. "Maybe you need to read that flashing sign, Mare, before your momma has a coronary."

"What does it say?" she asked, feeling confused. "I can't make it out, so just tell me."

Viv shot up in her seat, leaned over her mother's head, and yelled out through tears of laughter: "The sign says 'Come join us for Hebrew dancing'…and I cannot wait to see GiGi kicking her heels up with some Hebrew dancing tonight!" Falling back on the seat again, she giggled uncontrollably.

GiGi shot around in her seat. "Viv, pipe down! This is obviously a cult Mary has dragged us to! Look around you. Do you see these big families piling out of their vans dressed like the Amish? How in heaven's name is this funny?"

"Look at you wearing your size nothing Ann Taylor pants with that flashy sequin top among the Amish Hebrew dancers," she said, poking fun, "how is this *not* funny?"

"Mary," she said, "your sister, while uncouth, makes a good point. I am going to stand out like a big fat pig on slaughter day at this church, and in case you didn't get the memo, these folks hate pork, which means they will rip me to shreds as soon as I walk through the doors." Clearing her throat, she then became very serious. "Plus, I'm not entirely comfortable with Hebrew dancing, are you?"

Mary was watching the members of the fellowship walk into the building; they really did look like clones of one another. But she was determined. "Mom, we told the Dilbecks we'd come, so what's the harm in trying it out?" A smile broke out on her face as she continued, "Plus, if these people mistake you for a pig, I'll let them in on our little secret."

"What secret?" GiGi asked, honestly curious.

"That you are nothing more than a harmless high-fashion turkey." She snickered, altering her voice into the best imitation turkey she could do. "Gobble, gobble, gobble."

Even Poppy thought that was funny, but he knew better than to crack even a slight smile, so he remained stoic and held it back.

GiGi decided if she had to go to the bizarre Sabbath service, she would surely lead the way. So when they all entered the building, she went straight for the back row. "There is plenty of space for us right here." She smiled, pointing the way for her crew.

"Mary!" Brian Dilbeck shouted from the front row. "I've saved you all a seat with us." His face was beaming. "Please, come join us! There is room for all of you."

"Oh my dear Lord," GiGi whispered under her breath while waving big and friendly in Brian's direction. "I cannot believe our luck, Poppy"—she threw her bag over her shoulder and marched up to join the Dilbecks—"to have a front row seat for Hebrew dancing in Satan's cult sounds delightful, doesn't it?"

The sarcasm wasn't lost on Viv, who heard her mother and began laughing again. "I cannot even begin to tell you how ecstatic I am that I decided to tag along tonight."

"Shut up, Viv," her mother rejoined rather quickly.

All places of worship are typically arranged in a similar fashion. There is a stage for the worship leaders and the pastor, an altar for prayer, and seating arranged for people to gather. For the most part, the Lost Tribe Fellowship looked the same as any other church, even though it met in what used to be a retail plaza. Between the first row and the stage, however, was a great expanse of empty space. Unusual music piped loudly through the worship center, and GiGi, determined to know what she had gotten herself into, leaned over and shouted, "Brian!" He didn't hear her, so she tried again.

"Brian Dilbeck!" But he still couldn't hear her; the music was too loud.

Shaking her head in true disgust, she muttered, more for her own benefit, "Lord, even the Bionic Woman with her freakishly super-powered ears couldn't hear me over this booming music."

Not willing to give up, however, she leaned forward and practically yelled, "Brian! Good Lord, can you hear me?" He couldn't.

Tate finally got up from her seat to tug on the man's sleeve, pointing back toward her grandmother. Brian, in response, got up from his seat and knelt down before the matriarch of the family.

"Do you need something, GiGi?"

She despised that the man awkwardly kneeling in front of her felt comfortable enough to call her by her love name. She wanted to remind him that he was *not* family and to tell him to use her proper name but knew it would come off as haughty. And she was in a church, after all. "Yes, I have two questions. First, what is this loud music that's blaring through the speakers?"

Brian listened for a second and answered: "That particular song is called 'Yeshua,' and that is a small group called Lamb singing. It is beautiful, isn't it?"

"You don't understand what I am asking," GiGi said. "What *kind* of music is that?"

Brian smiled. He sort of felt pity for her, knowing his church was going to be different than anything she had ever experienced before. Her boundaries were getting ready to be shoved. "It is called Messianic music. Do you like it?"

"Not particularly. I prefer hymns and praise music myself, but to each his own," she answered sharply. "My other question is about this big empty space in front of us. Why are we pushed back so far from the stage?"

This time Brian giggled, taking GiGi off guard, offending her a little.

"Is my question funny to you?" she asked. "Because if you find it humorous, that was not my intention at all."

"No," he said, wiping his forehead with a handkerchief he pulled from his pocket, "but I don't want to give away everything." Brian stood, turned to shake Poppy's hand with a warm welcome, and returned to his seat.

"Well, that was odd," GiGi said out loud to no one in particular. "This whole place feels very strange to me."

Viv, seated to her left, on the other side of Tate, who was now propped beneath her grandmother's arm, spoke up: "It feels strange because it is a cult." Reaching over to pat her mom's knee, she continued, "For the record, I never dreamed I'd live to see the day my holy-roller mother darkened the doors of a cult, and now, here you are, front and center." Viv pulled back before her mother could slap her and began to shake with laughter again.

"Rise up to your feet!" A voice boomed from somewhere in back of the room. As one, the entire room stood. "Nightfall is upon us. Another Sabbath has passed. Oh, seed of Abraham, let us now praise and worship Yeshua with dance and song!"

A praise band leaped up on the stage and began playing a song as the aisles filled with men, women, teenagers, and children. They were all clapping, dancing, jumping, and shouting the words: Baruch Adonai Shout of El Shaddai. And the empty space before them was suddenly filled with dancers of every size, age, and color. They spun in perfect harmony, around and around, raising their hands just before dipping them again, in sync, together. Praising God with Hebrew dance.

Poppy, in shock over the suddenness of it all, felt his jaw nearly hit the floor. There he stood, with his mouth gaping wide open, as dancers flung their arms in front of him. Viv, who had never completely stopped giggling, burst out with full cackling laughter, imagining what a tough pill this was going to be for her mom to swallow, and she was correct. Poor GiGi stood in stone cold panic. She did manage to keep her head held high, attempting to cover up her true feelings, but the fact that she was carefully checking the pulse in her neck with her right hand while poking her husband with the other, gave her away.

"Poppy," she squeaked, trying to conceal her words through bright red lips that barely moved, "hold me up, baby, because I could be crashing down to the floor any second. My heart is racing so fast I can't keep count of it."

As if things couldn't get any worse, the unexpected happened when Tate and Wills stepped forward to join the circling dance. GiGi, in response, instinctively grabbed her heart and sat down with a thud, pulling her husband down with her. "We've lost them, Pops. Tate and Wills are dancing with the cult."

Poppy wished he could have disagreed with his bride, but he couldn't. By all appearances, it certainly seemed Mary and her children were being sucked right into the pandemonium. So they sat together, taking it all in. To pester them a bit more, Viv even jumped in and danced for one of the songs, leaning over her shoulder to wink at her parents every time she spun their way.

"Is it wrong for me to want to spit at her?" GiGi asked, but Poppy never answered. The truth was, he wanted to wring

Viv's neck for encouraging the whole thing. He kept turning to look at Mary with Miss Charity propped up on her lap. His daughter wiped continual tears from her face as the music played on. GiGi noticed, too. Both feared life was getting ready to take a major turn.

After several songs had played, and all the dancers were sufficiently worn out, Scott, the pastor, asked everyone to return to their seats. "Today's message," he began, "is about the power of Yahweh to create beauty from ashes, breathing new life into what was once dead."

The sermon was not a long one and was fairly simple to follow. He stuck to scripture, focusing primarily on the book of Isaiah, and actually made a lot of sense to GiGi and Poppy, who were expecting…well, they were expecting a cult. To end, Scott slammed his Bible shut and grasped each side of the podium as he worked into the grand finale that was to come.

"Who today believes Yahweh is a God who restores?" The pastor's voice was so loud, the words seemed to bounce off the walls.

The crowd, as one, chanted: "I do!"

"Who today believes Yahweh is a God who redeems?" he continued, raising the decibel level of his voice even more.

The crowd, again, shouted, raising their own voices even louder. "I do!"

"Who today believes Yahweh is a God who can take our sins and wash them away, leaving our hearts as white as snow?"

This time, the crowd stood and celebrated, with arms raised. "I do!" Mary jumped up with Little Miss and shouted with them.

The room fell quiet. Scott leaned up to the microphone and asked one simple question, as if he and Mary were the only two in the room. "Mary Montgomery, do you really believe that?"

"Yes, I do," she whispered.

GiGi and Poppy turned and looked at each other, eyes wide open, not believing the pastor was speaking directly to their daughter in the middle of a church service. Nothing remotely like that had ever happened in their church, and they had attended faithfully for years.

"Then turn around and face the back of the church," he said.

As Mary turned, the pastor continued to speak. "Today is the day for the sins of your family to be washed clean. Philip, what do you have to say before these witnesses?"

There he was, standing in the back of the room, tears streaming down his face. Mary gasped, still holding Miss Charity in her arms.

"Before these witnesses and my family," Philip shouted, "I want to ask forgiveness for my sins." He stepped out in the direction of Mary and continued to walk as he spoke. "I want my family to be restored, redeemed, and made new. I love you, Mary, and I am so sorry for hurting you." He was now directly in front of her, his eyes looking directly into hers. "Will you say your wedding vows with me again, this night, in front of all of these witnesses? Can we begin again? Can you forgive me?"

The room again fell silent. Wills and Tate looked on, daring to hope for a miracle. Miss Charity instinctively reached for her daddy, and he took her into his arms and held her tight, kissing her face, tears still falling from his eyes.

"Mary," he went on, "I have loved you my whole life. If you will give me another chance, I promise to prove to you that my repentance is real. I have turned away from the past and can only see my future with you and our family."

GiGi, Poppy, and Viv were floored. This, they never saw coming.

Scott, still at the podium, spoke up again. "Mary, have you ever sinned against Yahweh?"

Mary stood there, hearing every word spoken, yet still looking into the eyes of Philip. Silent.

Scott continued, "Scripture says all have sinned and have fallen short of the glory of Yahweh...so you must ask yourself…are Philip's sins greater than yours? Are his sins somehow unforgivable while your own sins are held to a different standard?"

"Stop it!" demanded GiGi.

"Stop speaking the truth?" Scott countered. "Never. I could do no such thing, even if I tried. Yeshua died on a cross to take away my sins. He forgave me even though I am undeserving. And because of His forgiveness, I must forgive others as freely as He forgave me. All of His followers must do the same in order to enter His everlasting Kingdom. Including Mary."

"Forgive me, Mary," Philip cried. "Please, for our family's sake, forgive me."

She still stood silently, eyes held in Philip's gaze.

"What do you have to say about it, Wills? Would you have your parents forgive each other?" Scott asked, knowing what the answer would be.

"Yes," answered Wills.

"Me, too," followed Tate, holding tightly to her brother's hand.

"Forgive him," someone chanted.

"Forgive him," another joined in.

Within seconds, the entire crowd rang out with one simple plea: "Forgive him."

They said it repeatedly until GiGi was so fed up, she couldn't help but take the matter into her own hands. Climbing up to stand on her chair, she turned toward the crowd and screamed from the top of her lungs: "Hush up! All of you! This is a private family matter, and not something to be paraded about like a circus act in front of a bunch of strangers who seem to believe they are holier than my family. I've been in church my whole life and have never witnessed such a spectacle."

"That's right," Viv chimed in, rising to stand on her own seat while placing her arm around her mother's back to steady her. "We are Christians who are saved by Jesus and don't need to be taught anything new from a bunch of Amish-looking people who are obviously in a cult."

A smile broke out across Scott's face. Their actions didn't anger him; they excited him. "Yes!" He clapped. "The devil is present, and he is trying to detour this reunion, which can only mean one thing! If you dare to trust Yahweh today by offering forgiveness to your husband, Mary, Miss Charity *will* be healed. This is a test, Mary! You must forgive Philip right now and defeat the enemy!"

"Forgive him! Forgive him! Forgive him!" the church began to chant again, ignoring GiGi and Viv's pronouncement.

Mary looked at Miss Charity, wrapped in her father's arms, and asked: "My baby will be healed? Are you sure?"

"It's a word from Yahweh, from me to you, sister," Scott replied. "I'm just a humble prophet of the King, charged with speaking His truth."

"Forgive him! Forgive him! Forgive him!" The words continued to ring out all around her. GiGi and Viv, still standing on their chairs, made their best attempt to squelch the crowd's chanting, but they were ignored. This group had one leader, and they were bent on following him.

Mary turned her eyes toward the pastor. He seemed absolutely confident that what he'd said was true. She then turned toward the Dilbeck family and caught Brian's face. He was nodding his head up and down with a big grin. Last, her eyes met those of Tate and Wills. She knew they wanted their family to be reunited more than anything. How could she not step out in faith for Miss Charity's sake? What did she really have to lose?

"Then yes," she announced, "I forgive you, Philip, and will renew my vows to you tonight."

Scott, in turn, pounded his fists on the podium, pointed at GiGi and Viv, and wailed: "Get thee behind me, Satan!"

Mary didn't notice when four ushers grabbed her parents and Viv by the arms and pulled them out of the sanctuary. She, too, had been ushered out to a private room where she would prepare to renew her vows to her husband, with Tate, Wills, Miss Charity, and the Lost Tribe Fellowship standing as witnesses.

Chapter 5

The following Monday morning was an atypical December day. Seventy-degree temperatures and bright sunshine ensured it would be a day for outside work and play. A couple of nights had passed since the ordeal at the Sabbath service, and the entire family was still reeling over the drama. The Dilbecks were an interesting crew. Refusing to eat pork and shellfish, going to church on Saturdays instead of Sundays, and using the name Yeshua made them different, but Mary couldn't get her mind off of how firmly they believed following the Old Testament rules would free her family from all of life's troubles and would bring healing to Miss Charity. It was a huge claim, an outlandish claim, but they stood by it without wavering. Wasn't that the type of faith John the Baptist and all the apostles preached? Were they not all out unabashedly promoting this kind of gospel to all who would hear?

"Mary." Preacher Walker's voice was always filled with joy. It was good to hear from him.

"Hey, Preacher!" Mary held the phone between her shoulder and ear. "What's up?" She was scrambling eggs on the stove top, getting ready to feed Wills before sending him off to school.

"Well, Jeannie and I wanted to stop by and see Miss Charity today. We've made y'all a slew of cookies. Would that be all right with you, dear?"

Mary thought about her experience at the Lost Tribe Fellowship service. Maybe it wouldn't hurt to talk to Preacher Walker about it, she thought. "Today would be a fabulous day for some of Jeannie's cookies." She grinned, excited about the possibility of telling them about all she had learned, especially about how Miss Charity was finally going to be healed.

Christmas was a little more than a couple of weeks away. By now, Mary normally had her house decorated from top to bottom, both inside and out, with white lights, jazzed-up Christmas trees, and a life-size nativity scene. But that was not the case this year. Hoping to rescue her daughter from Grinchville, however, GiGi had brought a twenty-four-inch-tall ceramic Christmas tree with colorful lights to Mary's house. The shiny little tree that had been passed down to her from her own mother stood alone on a table in the Ocoee Street home's front window as a pitiful reminder of what was traditionally a ten-foot-tall Christmas tree, but other than that, the house wasn't in celebration mode at all. After being filled in on all the latest happenings by the busiest busybody of the south, Preacher Walker and Jeannie hoped to change all that by bringing some holiday cheer back to the Montgomery home. At least that was the job GiGi had charged them with.

"So," Jeannie began after walking in the door with her husband not far behind, "we've come to visit Miss Miss, but we've also come with our work clothes on."

Mary was so happy to see them. "Work clothes?" she

asked, laughing. "What kind of work are we doing today?"

"Before we get to all that," Jeannie answered, "let me get my hands on that baby girl."

GiGi pulled the elder and his wife into the great room where Miss Charity was propped up on the sofa with pillows and her favorite blanket, watching Elmo. Mary got busy fixing them cups of coffee, decaf, with a little cream and sugar, as the rest of the group doted over the little one. Holding up her right index finger, Jeannie spontaneously knelt on the floor close to Miss Charity and began to sing: "This little light of mine, I'm gonna let it shine. This little light of mine, I'm gonna let it shine."

Preacher Walker and GiGi joined in. "This little light of mine, I'm gonna let it shine, let it shine, let it shine, let it shine." Miss Charity's face lit up like the sun. She reached up with open arms and was greeted with a gentle hug from Jeannie and a pat on the head from the preacher.

"Somebody is finally getting back to her old self," announced GiGi. "Watch her charming everyone around her with that sweet, happy face. She has my smile, don't you think?"

"No, I think it is perfectly clear that she has *my* smile," quipped Mary, flashing a sideways glance toward her mom. Then after delivering the coffee to her longtime friends, she found a comfy spot on the sofa and folded her legs up beneath her. "But you know what? She probably gets her feisty spirit from you, GiGi."

"And that's a good thing, darling," GiGi answered, "because it is my feisty spirit that has helped her become such a warrior princess." She jumped up to her feet, pumping her arms up and down like a prizefighter. "Ain't no heart surgery gonna to take us down, am I right, Miss Charity?"

GiGi then rushed over to Miss Charity, holding out one of her fists to Miss Charity, who met it with a bump of her own tiny, balled-up fist. A giggle filled the room, making everyone laugh. Miss Charity probably didn't understand what all of her GiGi's commotion was about, but the message was perfectly clear. Her grandma loved her a whole lot.

When coffee cups were empty and small talk had ended, Jeannie was the first to bring up the dreaded subject.

"Mary, we have a little surprise for you. We wore our work clothes today so we could help you put up your decorations." Clearing her throat, she obviously felt a bit nervous about the subject. "Won't it cheer Miss Charity up to see your big Christmas tree take the place of that puny little tree in the window?"

The preacher chimed right in, bearing a bright smile. "Yep, a Christmas tree just turns a house around and brings a special joy, don't it?" He got up, offered a hand to Jeannie, and continued, "I guess we better hop to it, old lady!"

She swatted him on the arm playfully. "Old lady?"

Both made a beeline for the kitchen with their coffee cups, hoping Mary would go right along with their plan.

"Well, about that," Mary began, following behind them, hoping they wouldn't give her too hard a time about the big changes being made in her life, "my family won't be celebrating Christmas this year. Are you aware the Bible forbids Christmas trees?"

That announcement was too much for GiGi. "Hush your mouth, Mary! Don't say that where baby girl can hear. What on earth is she supposed to do without the baby Jesus, a Christmas tree, and Santa Claus?"

Preacher Walker and Jeannie, feeling uncomfortable, didn't know what to say. This wasn't like the Mary they'd known for so many years. Like GiGi had warned, something was very wrong.

"Santa Claus represents Satan," Mary said, as if she were suddenly an authority on the subject. "Just change a few letters around and you'll find they're all there. Why do you think he wears the red suit?"

"I wear a gaudy red sport coat to church every year at Christmas time, but that don't make me one of Satan's workers, does it?" the preacher teased.

"Well, that's not all. Did you know Yeshua wasn't even

born in December? He was born in the fall. At Sukkoth. So we will be celebrating his birth next year at the right time, in a tent under the stars instead of around a pagan Christmas tree."

Preacher Walker's folksy voice usually set an even-keeled mood in almost any situation. He hoped today was no exception, because the tension between GiGi and her daughter was growing.

"Mary, Santa is fun for kids," he began. "The idea of him sparks their imaginations and makes the season a whole lot of extra fun. Satan wouldn't want any part of something that brings joy to little kids. Remember? He is the one who comes to steal, kill, and destroy." His eyes twinkled when he spoke. "And I hear your point about Jeremiah chapter ten and what it says about decorating a tree in your house being a sin, but those trees back then were cut down and used for idol worship." He sort of giggled. "I've never seen you bowing down to your Christmas tree, so I don't think that part of scripture applies here."

Mary listened, but she didn't hear. Her mind was made up.

"We aren't getting through to her, Pastor, and I'm sorry," GiGi said, glaring at Mary. "I know that look in my daughter's eyes, and she is not being moved by what you're saying. I had you and Jeannie come all the way over here because I thought you all might be able to crack a dent in her thick skull. But the more you try, the more determined she becomes." GiGi was clearly perturbed.

"I was the one who invited them over this morning, Mom," Mary responded, a bit put out herself. "Preacher Walker called and said he and Jeannie had made cookies for us, remember?"

"Of course I remember, because I set the whole gosh-darned thing up! I have been calling the poor preacher and Jeannie every single day since the Dilbeck Thanksgiving dinner fiasco to plot about how we can unite and save you from the Lost Tribe Fellowship voodoo." GiGi knew anger would get her nowhere with Mary, so she turned on the fake tears and pulled out her soap box.

"You can't see it, honey, but the Dilbeck family is luring you down a dangerous path. Before long you'll be wearing skirts down to your ankles, and that pains me, because you've always been so cute in your fashionable clothes." Dabbing her eyes with some tissue she found in her pocket, GiGi continued, "Are you sure you're ready to give up Christmas, Easter, pork, shellfish, and Saturdays, and for what? For salvation that is supposed to be a free gift? I can't believe you have bought into that new-fangled baloney because you think your actions will heal Miss Charity's heart. Lord sakes, girl, when did you start believing there was anything you could do to earn favor with God? Are you in control or is He?"

The rest of the visit went downhill from there. Mary was unflinching, GiGi would not stop preaching, and Preacher Walker and Jeannie, well, they pretty much became referees between the two.

Grasping onto a final thread of hope for her little girl's healing, Mary had convinced herself that the Lost Tribe Fellowship, and all of the onerous rituals that went along with it, held a miraculous key she'd been missing. She was determined to unlock the mysteries of God so her youngest child would have a healed heart. In the process, she even dared to bury memories of Bonnie Cutless and to put aside all the hurt Philip had caused.

This year, whether Mary's momma liked it or not, the baby Jesus was out, and a new-fangled, cult-concocted version of Hanukkah was in. Mary's spiral into the abysmal occult was now official.

Chapter 6

By the time March rolled around, Mary and her family were full-fledged members of the Lost Tribe Fellowship. At nightfall on Friday evenings, Sabbath began with the lighting of candles, the blessing over the candles, and a hearty meal including homemade challah bread…and then for twenty-four hours, the family turned off all electronics and rested, focusing on reading the Torah and prayer. This weekly practice was then punctuated by the Saturday evening services at the Lost Tribe Fellowship, where they all celebrated with Hebrew dancing. Only the faithful duo, GiGi and Poppy, remained at Preacher Walker and Jeannie's church, but they were also attending the Saturday "Sabbath" service with Mary's family, pretending to be interested. GiGi insisted they keep their eyes and ears open, just in case things got too out of hand.

Wills and Emma, meanwhile, became more serious. According to the fellowship's rules, they couldn't date but were allowed to practice courtship, which came with a long list of rules. Both had stood before the fellowship and publicly promised to abide by each step that had been preordained for the youth of the church as to courtship practices. The Lost Tribe Fellowship had maintained that following such arranged guidelines kept all parties pure and holy before the Father. And wanting to please both the fellowship and Emma's family, Wills had quickly jumped on board.

In addition, he had agreed to give up football, the sport that had not only provided him with a passion, but also with a goal. As far back as he could recall, he had wanted to play the sport on a college level. Now a junior in high school, he was giving it all up. For religion. For love. For Emma. The Sabbath began on Friday night once the moon made its presence known in the sky, which meant high above the Friday night lights, during the football games. So football was now forbidden.

"Suck it up, cupcake," Emma's father joked while giving him a condescending pat on the back, making Wills feel ashamed. "After all," Brian then suggested, "Yeshua gave His life for you when He was nailed to a cross. Surely, you can give up a silly football game for Him."

Wills had known, once those words were spoken, that he would never throw another official touchdown, call a play in a team huddle, or feel the high that can only come from victory after a nail-biting finish. One would have expected Brian Dilbeck to have some sort of sympathy for Wills since he had played high school football, and even a couple of years of college ball, but that was before Brian came to this "Messianic Lost Tribe of Israel" belief system. Wills sometimes secretly wished he had come into it *after* his glory days of football were behind him. It was too late, though, now.

"I'm so glad you could come meet me today, Wills," Brian said as he again patted his daughter's suitor on the back. The two had agreed to meet at the church building. Scott, the pastor, was there, too.

"Hello, Mr. Dilbeck and Pastor Scott." Wills greeted each man with a firm handshake. "How are you?"

"I hope you don't mind my asking the pastor to join us," Brian interjected, motioning for Wills to follow him to Scott's office.

It was midweek, and Wills had just finished a full day of school, so he was tired. Yawning, he fell back onto the massive leather sectional that wrapped around the far corner of the room before propping his feet up on a glass coffee table. Both Scott and Brian pulled up a chair to sit in front of him.

"This is a very important meeting, Wills," Brian began, "so please sit up and listen closely."

Wills wasn't prepared for a serious meeting and immediately felt unsettled. He had thought they might be offering him a leadership role in the fellowship, but this sounded urgent. Dropping his feet onto the floor, he leaned forward and planted his elbows on his knees. "Have I done something wrong?" he asked.

"No, it's just the opposite." Scott laughed. "You're doing everything right."

"Good," he said, sighing, "you scared me there for a minute." Wills felt the tension leave his body as he relaxed, now looking forward to this time with the two leaders of his church.

Scott and Brian watched as Wills settled back, loosening up again. Brian couldn't help but think of how Wills was getting ready to be stunned by what they had brought him in for. Unbeknownst to the teenage boy with the all-American good looks, the two elders had been anticipating this meeting for weeks. They had met about it, practiced what would be said, and were elated that the time had finally come. Brian, a smile radiating his face, gave a nod toward Scott. "Are we ready to begin?" He prepared to drop the bomb.

GiGi and Poppy, at the same time, were sitting at home having coffee on their back porch when Mary popped in with Tate and Miss Charity in tow. "Hey, Mom," she chirped, "I made you and Pops some homemade bread and some of my famous pimento cheese."

Both jumped up to greet Mary and the grandkids with hugs and kisses. "Mary," GiGi groaned, clearly unhappy to see Mary following the Lost Tribe Fellowship's code of dress, "if you want to dress like the Amish, that is one thing, but to take our cute Tater Bug and put her in these long sad-sack skirts is an absolute abomination."

It was true. Mary's family had transformed in the last several weeks. No longer wearing pants, each female had a closet full of what the Lost Tribe Fellowship deemed to be modest clothing. Most of it had been given to them by members of the group, and it all looked like it had come straight from a thrift shop.

"Can I at least take you girls shopping and buy some long skirts that appear somewhat up to date and from this century?" GiGi pleaded, holding Tate out at arm's length, giving her a good once-over. "I can't bear to see you all looking homeless in these hand-me-downs. It depresses me."

Tate, now trained on how to appropriately handle conflict by her new church leaders, responded with confidence: "It's important for us to not be materialistic, GiGi. We want to honor Yahweh with how we dress and want to put our money into things that build the eternal kingdom, not in things that will pass away like dust."

GiGi lifted her face to shake her head at Mary. This had gone too far.

"Tater Bug, don't you want to look young and modern?" she asked.

Tate, not wanting to be pulled into another long conversation about her family's beliefs with her grandparents, made her way toward the kitchen, pulling Miss Charity by the hand, to find a cookie. Just before disappearing out of sight, though, she replied with intention, "Yahweh cares about my inner beauty."

"Mary," GiGi blurted out, barely able to contain her disgust, "when did Tate decide to hang up her teenage years to become an old-timer cult priestess?"

"Don't even start, Mom," Mary interrupted, "you have to respect our beliefs or we won't be able to come around you. I've already told you that."

Acutely aware of the hold the Lost Tribe Fellowship now held over her daughter, GiGi shoved down her anger and quickly changed the subject. "Where is Wills? Didn't he want to come see us?"

"Of course he would want to see you, but he's busy at the church today."

"In the middle of the week? That's odd. What's he doing…scrubbing toilets? Washing windows? Acting as the general custodian for the two kings who believe they're too good to work?" GiGi's words were curt, but she didn't care. Brian and Scott paraded around the fellowship like they owned the place and all the people in it, and she was sick of it. "Oh, let me stop and think of the positive side of this," she continued. "Maybe if Wills cleans the church every week, Yahweh will heal Miss Charity's heart."

Mary, trying to manage her mom and dad, bit her tongue and didn't fire back, even though she wanted to. "No, he is not a custodian, but if they asked him to help clean the place, I know he would gladly do it. For your information, Scott and Brian asked him to meet them at the church so they could talk to him."

"Give me a break," GiGi muttered with disdain. "Neither one of those self-righteous men think their poop stinks.

They are lording over all of you, and this so-called meeting will be their way of pushing Wills into yet another part of the sick cult agenda." GiGi and Poppy were skeptical, and with good reason.

Meanwhile, Scott and Brian were working diligently to brush each stroke as they painted a picture with flowery words that would bewitch almost anyone as young as Wills. Flattery, while often corrupt, can be a useful weapon. In this case, it was a death knell. The first part of the meeting was spent discussing Wills's relationship with Emma as both elders commended him on how well he had faithfully followed the courtship rules. Next, they encouraged the lanky teenager to describe his feelings about Emma to them.

"I care about her a lot," he said. "We have fun together, and she is not like any other girl I've ever dated." He quickly corrected himself. "I mean, she is unlike any girl I've ever courted."

"Do you love her?" Scott asked. Brian, looking on, unconsciously bit his bottom lip, anxious for the answer.

Wills, not wanting to disappoint, responded quickly: "Yes, I do love her…in fact, I love her very much."

"That's what we hoped you'd say, Wills!" The men instantly stood, pulling Wills by the hand to stand with them. Embracing him with a warm hug, Scott added with raised eyebrows, "Now, son, we need to begin preparing for your wedding."

For the next couple of hours, the two men rambled off scripture, gave their spiel about church policy, and spoke of Yahweh's perfect will. When Wills pulled into his driveway, he paused to gather the courage needed to walk in the house and face his mother, however, as he entered, it dawned on him that he could not recall a single word. All he knew was that his wedding to Emma was being planned. Wills Montgomery was getting married.

Chapter 7

"Married?" Mary asked, trying to force her brain to think straight during the utter shock of the moment. "You'll still be a senior in high school next year, so how are you supposed to get married?"

Mary had been in the fellowship long enough to know how things worked. The kids didn't go to traditional school; instead, they were all homeschooled. It was one of the church rules, and not too far out for Mary, since she homeschooled Tate. However, things with Wills were different. He had already been in the school system for such a long time, so the members of the fellowship had made an exception for him. They had accepted it. But now, they wanted things to change.

And as far as the whole matter about getting married while you are young, Mary and Philip had both discussed how wonderful it would be for their own children to follow in the footsteps of the Lost Tribe Fellowship families, whose married children were extremely happy. They had already attended two weddings where the young couples shared their first kiss just as they were pronounced husband and wife. Sexual impurity had not been welcomed into those stories, and that was such an admirable thing in a culture where pornography and immorality was so prevalent. So why was the concept bothering her now?

"They want me to withdraw from school immediately to begin home study. And they're right; with me doing the work at home, I can be finished with all my credits in six months, or maybe even less if I work really hard."

"And then you'll marry Emma?" She was careful to ask the question without revealing her own apprehension and doubt.

"Sure," he answered. "Why wouldn't I? She is the most perfect person I have ever met," he added, half-trying to convince himself. "You just don't find girls like Emma. I think I'd be a fool not to marry her."

Philip was out of town on business, and Tate was busy playing with Miss Charity in a separate part of the house, so as soon as Wills took off up the stairs toward his bedroom, Mary made a quick call to her sister. "Viv, what would you do if I told you Wills is planning to marry Emma in the next several months?"

Viv, who had been warning Mary that her family was getting too heavily involved with the Lost Tribe fellowship, couldn't believe her ears. "Are you serious?"

"I can't talk right now, because I don't want Wills and Tate to hear me, but would you call Momma and ask her to meet you here at my house at five o'clock tomorrow morning?"

Viv was many things, but a morning person was definitely *not* one of those things. "Five freaking o'clock?" she grunted, clearly agitated. "Really?"

"Yes," Mary urged with little more than a whisper, "before Wills and Tate wake up in the morning, and before Chief gets back home."

The next morning couldn't arrive fast enough. Philip had called, but wanting to hash the matter out with her mother and sister first, which is routine for most Southern women, Mary decided to not bring up the subject with him. Sleep had avoided her altogether, so when the clock on her oven blinked five o'clock, Mary was already waiting at the front door, fully dressed, coffee cup in hand.

"I tried to warn you, Mary, but you wouldn't listen," GiGi began, marching into the Montgomery home in a state. "You have been playing with fire for way too long, and now you are dragging your family down in flames…straight to the pit of hell if you don't do something right now."

The three settled onto the king-size bed in the master bedroom, propped themselves up on pillows, and hoped they could speak without being heard, behind a locked door.

While Mary and her two-member posse were on their way to full blown panic, the Dilbeck family was up having a hearty breakfast, already busy planning a wedding. The entire family sat around the table as the head of the house slowly paced around each chair.

"Yahweh is good!" Brian announced, stopping to wrap his

arms around a very happy Emma. "He has sent our beautiful daughter a husband who has been found faithful to all of His laws and commandments."

Still smiling, Emma looked up at her father. She admired the man. If he thought she should marry Wills Montgomery, no one could stop her.

He would name the date, choose her dress, and along with her mother, would plan the event. To honor her father, she would choose to love Wills all the days of her life. It was the least she could do. In honoring her earthly father, of course, she was honoring her heavenly Father. It was the way she had been taught. The betrothal had now been spoken into existence, and therefore, ordained by the Creator of all good things. Emma was to become a bride.

If the morning was full of peace, love, and harmony at the Dilbeck compound, it was the exact opposite in the Ocoee Street home where Liv was on a roll. "How in the world is Wills even remotely ready to become a husband and father? This is all absurd. And laughable." Mary and GiGi sat quietly on the bed, both clearly shell shocked, neither having a clue what to do or say. Viv, seizing the moment, kept chattering. "We've all seen how everyone in that church pops out babies like a bunch of overly rambunctious bunnies. God help us all, Wills will have ten kids by the time he's thirty. Maybe we could arrange to have him kidnapped…not for a long period of time, of course…just for the next nine months or so." Looking back between her mother and Mary, she finally asked, "You two aren't saying much of anything. Didn't we get together to figure out how we can bust this thing up?"

GiGi, taking a deep breath, answered, "Yes, of course, and kidnapping is the answer."

"Well, at least I'm trying to talk it out. You may think kidnapping sounds farfetched right now, but when Wills is getting ready to walk down the aisle, you'll be wishing you had considered it."

"Don't you think I'd like to kidnap him, honey?" GiGi threw her arms up in the air. "I'd love to take him off to Hawaii where he could be surrounded by a bunch of gorgeous girls in bikinis who would take his mind off that homely Emma!"

Mary was listening but still not saying anything.

Viv spouted back, "Oh, but you love Emma, remember? As I recall, you couldn't say enough about what a wonderful girl she was. You encouraged this whole thing, which means you are partly to blame, you know? I was against it as soon as I saw that ungodly fifty-passenger van the Duggar Family Wannabes pulled up in."

"My fault?" GiGi was already feeling guilty, but to have the blame thrown in her face was too much. "How is this my fault? I was left here to take care of this family while Mary was at the hospital taking care of Miss Charity. I wasn't aware I had to do a background check on every

Tom, Dick, and Harry that waltzed through the door. Emma seemed like a nice girl."

"Are you telling me that you, the fashion queen of Cleveland, Tennessee, did not think her choice of clothing was a bit off for a teenage girl?" Viv countered. "That you didn't think there was something fishy about a teenage girl who wears skirts clear down to her ankles?"

Mary, still sitting silent, listened to the two bicker back and forth.

"I did think she needed a fashion intervention, yes. But you know me—I try not to judge anybody. The Good Book says to 'judge not, lest you be judged.'" GiGi was now in martyr mode. "If I am to be blamed for this marriage, however, I will carry the burden for the rest of my days. I'll carry it all, Mary, so you won't have to."

"Mary, for God's sake, the kids will be up soon. Are you going to say anything?" Viv was getting worried about her sister. Even though Mary was upset about Wills's announcement, both Viv and GiGi knew she was steeped heavily in the Lost Tribe Fellowship cult. Her whole family had changed drastically to adapt to the new belief system. Even Philip, who had once been acting the part in order to win his family back, had propelled to a position of leadership in the fellowship. His once clean-shaven face now sported a full beard while *tzitzit* hung low from his pants to remind him of God's laws.

Mary's face showed what she felt in her heart. "I don't know what to say. I've given Yahweh everything in order to get healing for Miss Charity. I've gladly given up Christmas, Easter, pork, and shellfish...I now carefully keep the Sabbath and all the holy days...I've grown my hair long and changed the way I dress...I've lost lifelong friends over this. And now He is asking me to give Him Wills?"

Viv and GiGi were aghast. They heard Mary's words, but couldn't believe *this* was how she was processing the matter.

"Maybe this is the final test of my faith. The one that will break down all the walls and bring complete healing to Miss Charity's heart," she continued, seeming to gather resolve for what was to come next in her life. "I'm Abraham and Wills is Isaac," she said, as if light in her mind was forcing out the darkness, "And maybe Yahweh is asking me to give up my firstborn son, my only son, to get this miracle of healing."

It was as if Viv and GiGi were watching the scene from *Gone with the Wind*, when Scarlett O'Hara picks up the dirt from Tara and stakes her claim on the future. Mary's eyes looked out into the distance, and covering her heart with her right hand, she proclaimed in that sweet Southern voice: "This is my final piece of the puzzle, I know it is. My miracle is on its way."

Viv and GiGi, dumbstruck by the sight, became keenly

aware that Mary believed this. As crazy as it sounded to the both of them, her words were her truth, and she was not going to be moved.

"I guess there is nothing left to say then," GiGi's voice was as light as a feather, belying all the turmoil inside her heart. "Viv, are you ready to go? I can't stick around while my daughter sends one of her little lambs off to the wolves' den."

Viv was in full agreement with her mom. She looked at Mary and felt sad. So much had changed so fast.

Once the two had left the house, GiGi grabbed Viv and made a confession. "Liquor has never touched these lips of mine, but your sister, if she keeps up this nonsense, may turn me to the drink. Pray for me, honey, your momma might be flirting with old Jim Beam soon."

Chapter 8

The local hospital was only minutes away from the Montgomery home, but this must have been a serious fall. When Jeannie called, she had told Mary they were at Erlanger Hospital in Chattanooga. Wills and Tate stayed home with Charity while she and Philip made a quick stop to pick up GiGi and Poppy before rushing to the hospital. Few details had been given. Preacher Walker, changing a set of light bulbs at the church, had fallen off a ladder and taken a bad spill. All they knew for sure was that his back was injured.

"How long has it been since you've seen the pastor and Jeannie?" GiGi asked as they pulled up on the interstate.

Mary, receiving the point loud and clear from her mother, didn't answer. They both knew it had been way too many weeks. When the pastor and his wife had challenged Mary's new beliefs, she had pulled away from them. As the Lost Tribe Fellowship had taught her, it was imperative to remove anything and anyone who might hinder her faith if she really wanted to get her miracle. Preacher Walker and Jeannie had become obstacles, so she had removed them. It seemed reasonable at the time, yet now she felt ashamed of the decision.

They all rode the rest of the way in silence, each deeply concerned about their pastor, who was just as much a part of their family as anyone. When they arrived, Jeannie greeted each of them with a big hug. "I am so sorry I've worried all of you," she cried. "After calling my kids, I just picked up the phone and called y'all."

"No, no, don't be sorry. We are so glad you called us," said Mary. "I've been thinking of you all a lot lately, and what better place to meet than a hospital, right?" She tried to bring levity to the situation, and Jeannie appreciated her effort.

"He's asked to see you, Mary," she professed, taking hold of Mary's hand. "Would you be up for that?"

Mary grinned. "Sure, I'm up for that…C'mon, Chief, let's go see him."

"No, Mary, he asked to see you by yourself." Jeannie looked up at Philip and gave him a wink. "Is that all right with you Philip?"

When Mary entered the room, Preacher Walker was attached to a few tubes and a heart monitor, but he was sitting up, looking spry. "Well, would you look at what the old tom cat dragged in," he teased.

After giving him a peck on the cheek, Mary took a seat on the side of his hospital bed and grabbed hold of his hand. "Doing tricks on a ladder, were you?"

"Yeah, you know me. I'm trying not to grow up too fast." He laughed.

"Seriously, are you going to be all right?" Mary asked.

"What if I told you I'm not going to be all right? What if I told you I needed a miracle? What would you do, Mary?"

"Oh my gosh…I can't believe this." Mary gasped. "What's wrong with you? What do you mean you're not going to be OK?"

Preacher Walker, the master spinner of stories, said, "Well, that doesn't really matter, does it? I mean, death is death, and we're all gonna die at some point. At least that's what history has proved to us so far." The wise elder paused for a moment before reeling her in. "Do you really believe you've found the key to everlasting life…I mean, everlasting life on this earth?"

Confused, Mary quickly answered, "No, what would make you think something like that?"

"I thought that was why you left my church."

Mary drilled him with a blank stare.

He added, trying to make sure he got his point across to an unsuspecting Mary, "Then please, tell me why you left me and my church. I think, as your former pastor, I deserve to know, don't you?"

Mary didn't know what to say. Collecting a few thoughts in her mind, she sat very still beside him for a moment. "I didn't want anything to get in the way of my faith, and the truth is, I felt like you and Jeannie were doubting me. Even a little bit of doubt can put a chink in my armor of faith…and could potentially take away Miss Charity's miracle. I can't let that happen."

"I'm sorry if we made you feel like we were doubting you, and I'm especially sorry if you felt we could be the ones to get in the way of that little angel's miracle." The pastor squeezed her hand and left it at that. Silence again fell upon the room, urging Mary to be the next one to speak.

"You know how important it is to me for Miss Charity to be healed, and I believe with all of my heart that I have found the key to that, so I have to go with it."

The pastor interrupted, "Oh good, now we're getting somewhere. It sounds like you *have* found the key to everlasting life here on earth. Think about it. If you've found the key to healing miracles, then praise the Lord, everybody can live and never die!"

Mary, quick witted, suddenly realized the old fox was setting a trap for her. The highly addictive dose of hope she had been fed by the cult ran deep in her veins, and her mind was not going to give it all up without a darned good fight. "Are you dying?" she asked curtly, not offering even an ounce of her usual social refinement.

"Did I say I was dying?" The teasing tone in his voice was something she typically enjoyed, but not today.

"I don't recall," she responded, "but something tells me you aren't."

The pastor breathed out a heavy sigh. "Mary, we've all been dying since the day we were born. I'm going to die someday, probably long before you...but make no mistake about it, you are going to die...and so will Miss Charity. All the faith in the world can't change that. I wish it could, but it can't. It's almost like you have come to believe that God is a big soda machine just waiting for you to add your meaningless quarters of works into...with the expectation that an icy cold Dr. Miracle will come out. It's a silly analogy you have heard me spout off many times, I know it is...but somebody's gotta help you see. If God could be controlled by our works, then He wouldn't be God."

Without a good-bye, Mary turned and fled from the room. The pastor would be sent home the next morning with a prescription of pain pills and orders to stay off ladders, especially the tall ones.

Chapter 9

Mary's visit with Preacher Walker left her ever more determined to get her miracle. Come hell or high water, she was going to prove the Almighty was Who she believed Him to be. No one would mock her once her miracle came to pass.

If she had kept the Sabbath set apart and holy in the past, Mary would now up the ante even more…giving up electricity for twenty-four hours each weekend wouldn't be that big of a deal. Sure, she would have to plan simple meals ahead of time. But they could eat bread, peanut butter, canned meat, and fruit one day a week. And candlelight would bring a nice change. She simply had to remind herself, it would certainly be worth all the inconvenience once Miss Charity's heart was healed.

In addition, she would start wearing a head covering. What did she have to lose? Up until this point, she had played around with head coverings, wearing them only occasionally, and perhaps that was the final domino she needed to make everything fall into place. Yes, she would definitely make a commitment to wear some type of head covering at all times. What had kept her from doing this before? Pride. And wasn't it pride that comes before a fall? She despised herself for being so weak. From now on, she would wholeheartedly submit to all scripture; she would do this to show her love and honor for Yahweh.

And last, there was the television. Becoming very careful to allow only media that honored their faith into their home and minds, Philip and Mary had cut the television back a lot. But wasn't there more they could do? Worldly commercials were difficult, if not impossible, to monitor. TV would have to be removed from the house completely. Scripture says that "narrow is the way, and few find it." Mary was willing to give up anything...perhaps even everything...to be one of those few. Miss Charity *would* be healed.

Since the Montgomerys no longer celebrated "pagan holidays," Easter was not on their radar when spring rolled around. In its place, they planned to celebrate the holy day of Passover. Wills, now homeschooled, took a big part in helping his parents prepare the meal. After all, very soon, he would be leading his own Passover meal as a husband to Emma. Trying to maintain some type of relationship with the family, GiGi and Poppy had agreed to give up Easter as well. They all met at the Montgomery home, along with the Dilbecks, for the Passover feast.

GiGi, trying to find a way to keep in touch with her daughter, traded in her Ann Taylor denim and her Ivanka Trump pumps for a long, full skirt, ballet flats, a turtleneck shirt, and a head covering. Viv met her parents at their house, planning to ride with them. "I agreed to wear the long skirt, Mom, but I will not wear that hideous little lace doily on my head."

It didn't take much for GiGi, who was already feeling the pressure of what the day would hold for them, to become bent out of shape. "Listen, Viv, either put the doily on your head or don't go. Look at me; do you think I want to wear a doily? If I am willing to put myself out there, then you can do it, too. These are desperate times, and if we want to keep the lines of communication open with your sister, we have to conform to this nonsense."

Viv balanced the cream-colored lace patch on top of her head and looked at her reflection in the microwave oven door. "I don't get it. Why would Mary think something like this is important to God?"

"She is in a cult!" GiGi exploded, startling Viv. *"And they own her!"*

Pausing for a second to reflect on her own words, she gathered more steam and stomped her feet on the floor with two thunderous thumps.

"Theyyy owwwwnnnn herrr!" she growled with boiling fury.

Viv turned to her mother, who was wound up tight and holding two bobby pins. Swiping them in anger, she pinned the doily to her hair. "I still can't believe this is happening, but you're right. If I have to wear a doily to see my sister, well, I'll wear the stinking doily."

"Of course I'm right," GiGi grunted, coming down from her high horse and getting a glance of her own reflection in the microwave. "Why else would I go out in public dressed like a complete fool?"

Viv grabbed her purse and interlocked her fingers with her momma's. Honest to goodness sorrow filled her eyes. "How long are we going to go along with this act, anyway?"

Poppy, who had been tying *tzitzit* to his belt loop, chimed in: "As long as it takes."

When the three misfits arrived at the Ocoee Street home, they found the Dilbecks already seated around the table. Having been accustomed to Easter eggs, bunnies, fancy pastel-colored attire, and a honey-baked ham, they were immediately disappointed by the solemn nature of the occasion. Gigi, though, desperate to fit in, had studied all about the Seder meal and felt ready to go with the flow. This was the moment she'd been rehearsing; her audience was waiting, even though they didn't know it yet.

Placing her hands in a praying position under her chin, the petite fashionista, now dressed like an Amish woman, slowly walked toward the table and announced with a startling boom: "Here we are, the descendants of Abraham, gathering together to celebrate the day we were rescued out of Egypt by the hand of Yahweh!"

The look on everyone's face, including the face of her own husband, who had no idea she had planned such a thing, was priceless.

Dramatically sweeping her wide-open hands back and forth in front of her, palms facing them all, she continued: "He brought on the plagues because those Egyptians were a stubborn, heathen people." She then slowed down her cadence, holding up a single finger to carefully count each plague that she could recall: "He turned the water to blood…sent the slimy frogs…gave them all lice…and boils…and did a whole bunch of other frightening things before He sent the death angel."

"*Bam!*" She clapped her hands. Some of the younger children jumped with a start, but she trudged on, unhindered. "If you didn't have the blood on your door, the death angel killed the firstborn in each family…squashed 'em dead as a fly caught off guard by a swatter."

Pausing for effect, she brought her voice down to a gentle whisper. "And finally, those evil Egyptians let us go."

All eyes were fixed on her. In an effort to be charismatic, in a churchy sort of way, she spread her arms wide apart with great zeal and held them up in the air, bringing her voice up again, to a full grandiose level. "Praise Yahweh. He parted the Red Sea and commanded us to cross over. And so we obeyed Him and crossed over."

As she spoke, she took big steps, holding her lengthy skirt up with both hands and marching her knees up high with each step, pretending to walk excitedly over the dry land. Then, for the grand finale, she placed her folded hands up beside her face, and laid her head gently against them to imitate sleeping. "So we slept in the desert and trusted Him to provide us with food from heaven."

Pacing around the table, looking each person directly in the eyes, her voice crescendoed again into full volume. "And that's why we are here today, isn't it? We are *not* going to celebrate the pagan holiday of Easter with all of the bunny-rabbit symbols of fertility. We are *not* going to eat honey-glazed ham, because we now know it is unclean! And we are *not* going to be eating bread today, either." Looking over at the buffet table, she pointed in the general direction of the matzo crackers. "But today we will remember how Yahweh rescued us by eating the unleavened manna from heaven that has been prepared by Mary through the very hand of Yahweh."

To close, she took a bow…more of a curtsy…and took her seat in the lone empty chair. Stunned by the spectacle, and not knowing how to react, the Dilbecks looked down at the table. But not Viv. She applauded her mother's efforts and motioned for everyone else to join in. They eventually did. And in response, GiGi stood and gave another, very humble, curtsy.

Chapter 10

GiGi, Poppy, and Viv halfheartedly participated in the pomp and circumstance as the evening progressed. They tasted the bitter herbs, representing the bitterness of slavery; ate the *charoseth*, symbolizing the mortar used by the Hebrew people in the construction of buildings when they were slaves; and finally, partook of the *karpas*, celery dipped in salt water, which denotes hope and redemption. The evening was formal and planned, well executed, but not fun. At all.

When the Dilbeck gang left, GiGi offered to help her daughter clean up, actually planning, though, to get the latest scoop on Wills and Emma. Grabbing the dirty dishes, she placed them in the sink and turned on the water: "So, honey, your Passover Seder was nice. I have to admit, though, I prefer the Easter food more, even though I know Easter is satanic."

Mary, transferring the leftovers into plastic storage containers, was quick to clarify: "Calling Easter 'satanic' is a bit brash. I'd say Passover is the way Yahweh intended, especially since He spelled it out for us so clearly in scripture, but that man switched it up and distorted it to fit in better with what society wanted."

"Well, that's just Satan's way, isn't it? He sneaks in and distorts the scriptures to trick us all." GiGi, hoping to win Mary over by agreeing with her, nervously scrubbed the dishes with a soapy sponge, trying to remain believable.

"Here I've been putting bunny rabbits and bright-colored eggs all over my house during the spring, thinking I was celebrating the resurrection of Jesus when I was actually worshipping a fertility goddess." She scrubbed the dishes even faster. "It makes me almost vomit in my mouth to think about how I've disgraced my family and Yahweh all these years."

Viv popped into the kitchen to join the conversation. "Well, Mom, none of us knew. I don't think the Lord will hold us accountable for what we didn't know."

"Oh, yes He will!" Mary retorted, making her point loud and clear. "Our fellowship says we are all expected to read the Word and to allow the Spirit to speak to our hearts instead of letting traditions lead us to hell. So we can never use the excuse that we just didn't know any better. That won't fly with Yahweh."

"What about His grace and mercy, Mare?" asked Viv, actually curious about her sister's viewpoint.

Mary, pleased to see her sister warming up to the ways of her fellowship, smiled warmly. "Of course our Father is full of never-ending grace and mercy, but we must first repent of all of our wrongdoings. We need to name them, all of them, and then ask Him to forgive us. Have you asked Him to forgive you for celebrating Easter? And for forgetting His holy day of Passover?"

GiGi and Viv were now in a pickle, and GiGi was not too

happy that Viv put them in a position to lie. She was willing to pretend to go along with the cult to retain a relationship with her daughter and grandchildren, but outright lying was beneath her. She bit her lip and shot an evil glance toward Viv, who was more than willing to lie: "I've just repented in my heart…right now…this instant."

In response, Mary put her plastic containers down, rushed to her sister, and hugged her tight. "Then you are forgiven, Viv. Praise Yahweh!"

Turning in the direction of her mother, Mary asked: "Momma, have you repented?"

"Well…" GiGi pulled her hands back from the sink and dropped a plate on the floor. The crash was so loud and sudden, everyone came running to the kitchen to see what had happened. "I am getting so clumsy. Don't worry guys, it's just old Grandma making a big boob of herself in the kitchen. Now get back to whatever you all were doing and let me clean up my own mess."

Mary, grabbing a broom and dustpan from a nearby closet, offered a hand, but GiGi insisted on clearing the mess herself. "Honey, I don't mean to pry, but I was just wondering where we are on the impending wedding plans." She turned her back on Viv and Mary to gently tap the dustpan's contents into the garbage can, hoping the change of subject wasn't too obvious.

"Well," Mary answered, "since Wills is the groom, we

aren't doing any planning at all. His future in-laws, with help from friends at the fellowship, of course, are planning the entire thing. When Tate gets married, it will be my time to plan." Mary's smile gleamed like a schoolgirl's, which only added to her mother's growing agitation. As if Easter wasn't a complete bust, now her grandson was being dragged down the aisle by a psycho cult. Those were her thoughts, anyway.

When a call came just a few minutes later, Philip grabbed Wills and took off to the Lost Tribe Fellowship. Poppy had offered to join them, but Philip had asked him to stay back with all the females. Within the span of one hour, the police were standing at Mary's door. No one could have anticipated the evening would take such a turn.

Philip and Wills, when they arrived at the Lost Tribe fellowship building, had found vandalism beyond description. The outside brick had been spray painted with anti-Semitic language and symbols. Breaking in through a window, the vandals had dumped garbage cans full of urine all over the carpet and had smeared feces across the walls. A banner, bearing the Star of David that once hung across the front of the worship center, was now ripped to shreds.

But most disturbing was the message left behind, scrawled wildly on the walls, which read: "Jews, we will hunt your families down and make you wish you had never come to our Christian town."

Father and son were asked to follow the police to the

station to be questioned about what they had found when they arrived. Both were really shaken up, shocked by the damage that had been done. The police officer, at Philip's request, had gone to check on his family and to warn them to be cautious.

"Jews?" GiGi asked the policeman as she peered over Mary's shoulder, listening to the conversation. "That fellowship is obviously not a synagogue. It's more of a plaza, and not a nice one at that."

"I thought the same thing," the policeman replied, "but make no mistake about it, the damage speaks for itself…these vandals are serious about the threat. Whether you all are Jews or not makes no difference at this point. They think you are, so you all do need to be cautious. As you've already guessed, this has all the signs of a hate crime."

When the officer left, Mary settled Miss Charity and Tate down in her bed, allowing them to watch a favorite movie. Meanwhile, she motioned for her parents and Viv to join her again in the kitchen. She had news to share.

"Listen, Brian and Scott confided in Philip a few weeks ago about a phone call Scott received from a stranger," she whispered. "The person never gave his name, and the call came in as a private call with no return number. The caller was asking questions about the fellowship and the call quickly became antagonistic. I don't know all of the details, but I do know it worried both Brian and Scott. Both believe it is time for us to all consider selling our homes and form our own community…so we can support one another and remain more anonymous."

Mary spoke as if the solution were as plain as the noses on their faces. GiGi and Viv replied as one, in perfect unison: "A commune?"

GiGi, Poppy, and Viv were at a loss. They had waited around for Philip and Wills to return, listened as they recounted their disgust over the destruction they'd found at the fellowship's building, and then felt helpless as the two adamantly agreed with Mary. According to Philip, it was indeed time for the family to consider moving out of their home, at least on a part time basis, and to begin building a place of refuge on the planned communal farmland. This had become a matter of "standing up for what they believed in," "banding together," and "remaining safe." GiGi, normally a fighting force, knew better than to question the proposal. To have done so would have been to draw a line in the sand. Their beliefs had become like two passing ships in the night. Waves crashing up and down, against them both, were carrying them farther and farther apart. GiGi was looking for God's heavenly lighthouse to flash a beam of light, drawing them back together, but the matter was feeling like a lost cause.

Chapter 11

Emma wasn't eavesdropping when she accidentally happened upon a conversation between Scott and her father. "We definitely pulled it off," her father bragged. "Philip is in our hip pocket now."

"Yeah, I think he'll do anything to protect himself," Scott said. "That's at least one thing we have in common with him."

The two men were tinkering on an old truck out in the garage when the young teenager had decided to hunt for some craft supplies in the attic above. Hearing the name of her future father-in-law, she gently closed the attic's door and sat quietly, taking in as much as her ears would allow.

"You're right," Brian replied, "but we have to act fast. Mary and Philip have been in that old house for a long time, so it won't be easy for them to let go of it. We have to use fear, and then possibly more fear, to push them."

Scott's voice was muffled, but Emma clearly heard his response. "We don't necessarily need him to move out of that house. We just need to push him toward the idea of financially supporting the commune. We'll make him a modern-day George Bailey, helping out all the poor folk in our fellowship.

"That jack-leg can afford to have two homes, you know…and as long as he plans for one of them to be out on the farm, I really don't care."

The statement that followed perplexed her, frightened her even. "Well, our next move should get the job done." It was her father's voice.

Most teenage girls have a friend they can talk to, but not Emma. Homeschooled from the age of five, she had never been allowed to have friends outside the fellowship. Connected to the rest of the world by a fifteen-hundred-foot-long gravel driveway, her family's home was surrounded by more than one hundred acres of farmland. Having neighbor friends was not an option.

According to courtship rules, the young couple's texts were read by their parents. In addition, all phone calls were monitored. And of course, the two were not allowed to be on a date without a constant chaperone. Even if Emma wanted to tell Wills about the conversation she'd overheard, she knew it would be impossible.

A few days later, every key member of the Lost Tribe Fellowship awoke to find a swastika symbol spray-painted on his or her front door. It made the local news, and some were sure it would reach national attention at some point. Emma watched as her dad feigned surprise. Her mother fell for the act, and so did all of her siblings. But she knew. Her dad's plans, whatever they were, were now in action.

GiGi and Poppy rushed over to the Ocoee Street house as soon as they received word of the vandalism. They shouldn't have been surprised, given the "hate crime" comment made by the police officer, but they were. Things like this didn't happen in their Christian town.

"Mary," cried GiGi, aghast, "this has gone way too far. We are now teetering in some mighty dangerous territory. You have to wake up and get the hell out of this cult." Her mother was not one to curse, but when pushed to the limit, she could sling a few. "Pardon my French, baby girl, but I am shaken to my core." Holding a takeout menu from a local Chinese restaurant, she couldn't fan herself fast enough. With each flap of the makeshift fan, her bangs flew up and down, making the beet red in her cheeks show up even more.

"I agree," said Poppy. "We've gone along with this charade long enough."

Mary, standing in the front yard alongside her parents, all peering at the swastika symbol that now degraded the doorway on her beautiful old home, was perplexed. Up until this moment, she had actually believed her parents were close to joining the group. "What charade?" she asked. "And a cult? Really?" If she'd had a rock in her hand, she probably would have thrown it at one of them…just before kicking the other. "My family is in obvious danger…hello? Can't you see that horrid symbol on my front door? And we aren't the only targets, either. It has happened to a lot of us."

"Of course you're all in danger! Every last one of you!

Whoever did this is completely crazy!" answered GiGi, shouting in a very high-pitched shrill voice. "But it's your fault for dragging your family into all this nonsense. This swastika," she explained, pointing at the symbol on the door, "is on you!"

"Oh, I see…" If Mary was heated before, she was boiling now. "This is somehow my fault. How is it everything always ends up being my fault? Did I paint a hate symbol on my door? No, I didn't. Did I know someone was going to come out and vandalize my home? No, I didn't. For once, I can honestly say, this is something that is *not* my fault!"

"Wake up! Yes, this is absolutely your fault!" GiGi screamed. "You were the one who allowed yourself to forget your upbringing and become bewitched by Brian Dilbeck's trickery. He weaved and bobbed around the Bible, throwing in a lot of truth along with bits and pieces of downright lies, to make you believe if you did things the cult way, you'd get a miracle. And where has it gotten you, Mary?"

Mary was about to reply. Locked and loaded, she was ready to let her parents have it. However, before she could interject, her dad pounced right in.

"Your momma is absolutely right about this. You knew better. You've been raised in the church and knew better than to allow yourself to get into a cult. And we're to blame, too, for going along with it all. I can almost hear that darned Dilbeck right now. He'll be telling you that this vandalism proves how you all need to go move out to a commune together straightaway. And he'll probably suggest his farm. Why not? You can all haul out your doublewides and shotguns and then pay him rent to stay there. Before long, he'll have his place paid off. That's right. I believe he is an evil schemer with a plan to con all of you, and he's willing to use God to do it."

"He's like Jim Jones," GiGi shouted with panic, as if the truth had just dawned on her. "As soon as he has that land paid off, he'll be giving you all Kool-Aid to drink. Whatever you do, please, don't drink it!"

Mary's heart was racing. Philip was out of town, so she had called her parents for support, but all she was getting from them was condemnation. "You are both crazy; honestly, I don't know what to think." Mary was not only mad; she was also hurt. Her parents had rejected her new beliefs, and in doing so, had rejected her. "You need to leave or you're going to upset the kids. You have already disturbed me beyond belief and have crossed some major lines. And lest you forget, your grandson is betrothed to Jim Jones's daughter."

Stomping up the front steps, she jerked the front door open with such force it knocked her back on her heels. Just before slamming it shut to make her final point, she got in one more jab: "And make no mistake about it, we *will* be serving Kool-Aid at the wedding!" *Bam!* The door closed with such force, it seemed to shake the old house.

Every fiber in GiGi's body wanted to drag her daughter out of the house along with her grandkids and haul them off to a secluded island, far away from the Lost Tribe Fellowship. She knew, though, that it was too late. Her daughter had chosen the cult over her.

"Pops, we've lost her."

"Sugar," he replied, wrapping his arms around her, enveloping her into his chest, "I'm afraid we've lost them all."

On the way back home, the wheels in GiGi's head were turning. She had to think of a way to keep contact with her daughter and grandkids, so when the idea came, she knew it was sheer genius. Mary knew that she and Poppy had been pretending to be a part of the cult, but she had no idea that Viv had been pretending. The future of the family now lay on the shoulders of Mary's willful sister. It would require a lot of work, but GiGi felt hopeful about getting her other daughter prepared for the task ahead. A smile brightened her face.

"I've got this, Pops." She reached over and patted his leg as they entered their neighborhood. "I think I've actually got a plan that is sure to work!"

Her husband of many, many years shot her a quick grin. He didn't know what the old bird had hidden up her sleeve, and he didn't care. "You do whatever it takes, do you hear me?"

"Loud and clear," she answered with spunk, ready to outmaneuver Mary, Philip, and the whole gosh-darn cult.

GiGi was back in action.

Chapter 12

Brian and Scott's plan was underway. At $25,000 per acre, they would rake in a boatload of money from the unsuspecting fellowship. The new "subdivision" had been preapproved by the county years ago, and since the farm could accommodate about thirty single-family homes, the fellowship's leaders were singing a song to the tune of about seven hundred and fifty big ones. Add that to the money they received weekly in tithes and offerings, and the old high school buddies were set. For life.

Brian and Scott couldn't recall a time when they weren't the best of friends. They'd even attended college together where they were roommates. Scott, a psychology major, had studied Adolf Hitler and the Holocaust. He spent hours upon hours pondering how someone who was eventually determined to be a madman could lead an unfathomable religious revolt that claimed the lives of six million men, women, and children. Brian wasn't a psych major. In fact, his ambition, at that time, was to be a physical education teacher. But he listened, every day, to Scott's thoughts on the subject of Hitler.

"If one man could lead many men to slaughter people in the name of religion, why couldn't a man lead many men to give up money in the name of religion?" he had suggested many years ago. And it stuck. The thought, in fact, had led the two friends to dig more. While other students were out partying, they studied religion, primarily cults, to discover who the cult leaders had targeted, how they had managed to pull their followers in, and even mistakes they had made. It was now twenty years in the making, and their plans were finally unfolding. Both had decided, a long time ago, the way to make the most money with the least amount of work was through religion. Their wives and children were pawns, but wasn't that the way of the cult? Using people was a crucial component in getting what they wanted. And what they wanted was money. Lots of it.

"Landing Philip was key, wasn't it?" Scott asked Brian on the car ride over to the Montgomery home as both planned to pull Philip over into their court.

Brian laughed. "Yeah, who would have ever dreamed that fat-cat catch would come by way of one of my offspring?" He shook his head at the thought of it. "The mighty Philip Montgomery with the mongoloid kid has an affair with the biggest slut in town. Who would have ever bet on that? Not me...not in a million years." He was giddy. "But here we are, and his transgressions shall be our gain."

Scott hammered his fist down on the dashboard and mocked God. "In the name of Yeshua! His transgressions shall be our gain!"

The two continued to laugh. They had deceived everyone. Or so they believed.

It was dinnertime when Viv, Preacher Walker, and Jeannie arrived at GiGi and Poppy's home. GiGi, ever the hostess, had cooked a baked ham. For the rest of her days, she'd proclaimed, she would have ham at least once a week, if only to spite those devilish Dilbecks. The preacher had been filled in on all the latest details, so he had an idea of what to expect from the dinner invitation. But with this group, one never really knew.

"Now that we're all gathered, Pastor, could you bless our food?" Poppy asked, removing his ball cap.

An angel was in the room, but no one could see him. He wasn't there to impose, but to offer support. Unbeknownst to anyone in the room, Preacher Walker had been praying and fasting for the Montgomery family for weeks. And God the Father, ever faithful, had heard.

"Heavenly Father," he began, "the author Who has written every story in our lives, thank You for this time to come together and eat food that has been provided by Your hand. I pray that You will bless it and sanctify it, Lord. And as we eat together, will You open our minds to Your leading? Above all else, we want to magnify Your name. In Jesus's name I pray. Amen."

GiGi insisted on filling each plate. She doled out ham, potato salad, fried okra, baked beans, and fresh-baked rolls. No one could argue; the woman was an amazing cook.

As soon as everyone was seated, she sat at the head of the

table, ready to give her speech. Perched at her right side stood the angel; he leaned against a dining room window, looking forward to hearing all GiGi had to say.

"As you all know, Poppy and I brought you here so we could plan out a last-ditch effort to save the family from the cult. I can't believe things have become so crummy, but they have, and it will not do any good for us to bury our heads in the sand." Everyone ate as they listened, prepared for her to ramble on for a long while. "Viv is our secret weapon. As far as we know, Mary still believes Viv has bought into the Lost Tribe Fellowship hogwash. If she has to move out to the commune to keep her ears and eyes open for an opportunity to bust Mary and the kids out of there, well, that's a sacrifice she'll have to make."

Viv, who was happily eating her food, looked up and raised her hand. "I can't move out to a commune, Mother. I have a job. I work to support myself. Remember?"

"Did you not hear me? You are the secret weapon. You are the last-ditch effort. What is more important? Mary's family drinking the Kool-Aid and dying *or* your job?" GiGi was not going to back down. That much was obvious.

"Now," she continued, "what I'm thinking is that Viv's cover would be much stronger if she started dating one of the bearded men in the cult. Let's put that on the table for discussion. Who agrees?"

Once again, Viv raised her hand. "No one agrees."

"Do you believe it would make your cover stronger?" GiGi shot back, as sure of herself as ever.

"Probably…but I'm *not* going to date one of those cult men." Viv was horrified. Slapping her fork down hard on the table, she said, "I'd rather Mary drink the Kool-Aid. Honestly, I would."

Poppy had hoped his wife could be reasonable but realized it had been wishful thinking. "GiGi, we can't ask Viv to move to a commune, and we certainly can't expect her to pretend to date one of the cult members. It wouldn't be right. We are in a mess and it is beginning to look dangerous, but we can't act rash. We have to calm down and think, and let's try to be sensible." As he spoke the words, he knew he might as well be talking to a wall. She wasn't going to listen. Mary was her baby, and Wills, Tate, and Miss Charity her grandkids. For her, this was war.

Preacher Walker and Jeannie sat silent. He prayed quietly in his heart as GiGi and Viv continued to argue. The angel, patiently standing by, made his way to the older gentleman with the shock of white hair, and leaning over to his ear, he whispered four words: "Wait upon the Lord."

The words were so clear to the old pastor. He tried not to speak, fully intending to allow those who were talking to finish their thoughts…to wait for a pause in the ongoing, very present conversation…however, his mouth opened and he announced: "Wait upon the Lord!" The words surprised him. He heard the sound of his voice and knew the words had come from his mouth, but he had not initiated them.

Poppy and Jeannie turned to look at him as GiGi and Viv continued bantering with each other. "Wait upon the Lord!" He spoke again, this time with bold and fierce articulation, counter to his gentle personality. The room grew quiet; he had all of their attention. The angel, standing directly behind him, put his mouth once more to the old man's ear. The pastor repeated each word being whispered into his ear:

"Wait for the Lord! Be strong and take courage! Wait patiently for Him to accomplish His work. Do not fret because of him who prospers in his way, because of the men who carry out wicked schemes. Yes, wait for the Lord!"

GiGi, still seated at the head of the table, began to shake and whimper. Soon, they were all weeping as the Heavenly Spirit permeated the room, filling each and every space. Peace unleashed, took over, and wrought them all powerless. Somehow they knew these words were not from Preacher Walker but were words from the Lord to them. No one, however, knew it more than the elder gentleman, the one with the gentle soul, the clay that had been skillfully molded by many years of toil and strife so he could be used, this day, by the King of Kings. If he had ever doubted in the existence of God, he would never doubt another day in his life.

The angel rose up to leave but instinctively bent back down to touch the pastor's back. Rubbing his hands from the man's shoulders down to his lower back, with hands wide open, the angel brought life back into what was worn and broken, repairing his discs completely. In an instant, the pastor felt the chronic pain exit his body. Then, before vanishing, the angel of the Lord planted a kiss on top of Preacher Walker's downy soft hair and said: "Well done, faithful servant."

Chapter 13

GiGi heard the words of her pastor, and while she earnestly believed them to be words from the Lord Himself, waiting on the Lord went entirely against her makeup. She wasn't really one for stillness and calm, and she couldn't help it. In fact, in her heart, she blamed God for creating her to be such a fighting force who preferred response and action. So after the pastor and Jeannie left, GiGi backed Viv into a corner, demanding she follow her plan. Viv, seeing desperation in her mother's face, did what any child would do for a parent. She agreed to go along with the outlandish plan and would find a cult member to seduce, in a holy sort of way, of course. From now on, she would only be seen wearing those hideous long skirts with a doily on her head. Tomorrow was a new day. It was the day they would begin to aggressively take their family back.

Sam was his name. Sam Smith. Such an ordinary name for an even more ordinary human being. He laid wood floors, for crying out loud. How much more mundane could an occupation be? But he was single and Viv's age. It was him or no one. So, it was him.

"Sam?" Viv called the number she found on the Internet. "This is Viv from fellowship. My parents need to have their wood floors refinished, and I thought I would give them that as an anniversary gift. Could you please call me when you get this message so we can set up a time to meet at their house? Thank you! And many blessings to you!"

The message was friendly, but a bit more than buddy-buddy. She was a female, after all, and knew how to throw in a dab of flirtation. Within minutes, the wanton bachelor had called her back, proving he was beyond desperate for a mate. She laughed to herself as she considered her mother's plan. This would be scandalous. If she wanted to succeed, it had to be.

GiGi had filled Poppy in on most of the plan; she had to leave out the juicy parts or he would have disapproved, probably pitched a fit. The sky was unblemished by clouds when Sam arrived for dinner, leaving the sky sprinkled with plenty of stardust. If romance wasn't in the air tonight, it was missing a supreme opportunity. Even though Poppy felt uneasy about the shenanigans proposed by his wife, she had convinced him the plan was foolproof and that no one, especially poor Sam, would get hurt. "We have to do something," she had said. "How are we going to deal with it when our grandkids are living out on a commune in the middle of nowhere?" Not wanting to quarrel or to add any further commotion to an already tumultuous circumstance, he had reluctantly agreed to let her have her way. In return, she had promised to keep him in the loop on every detail. She had lied. It wasn't the first time and would certainly not be the last. In her mind, all was always fair in love and war.

"GiGi, Sam's here." Pops ushered Sam into the great room and asked him to take a seat. The three sat for several minutes, discussing the sand and finish wood floors in the house and what it would take to refinish them, when finally, Viv appeared. To her mother, she looked like an Amish nightmare, but they all knew Sam would find her irresistible. He was midsentence when she entered and lost his train of thought completely. Staring, fixated upon the vision of beauty, he was smitten. If GiGi were taking notes, and make no mistake about it, the bird was taking notes in her brain, this was a huge check off her list. As suspected, Sam Smith was in the bag.

They had dinner, because GiGi, still old-fashioned in some of her thinking, believed the best way to win over a man was by giving him good food for his hungry belly. Sam has worked all day, so he was starved. After two platefuls of roast, he finally took a breath. "Thank you for having me over and for considering me for this project. I'd like to begin right away if it's all right with you, and if I could work at night, after my official hours, I would like to do it as a gift to you."

"A gift?" GiGi eyeballed him, trying to figure out if he had an angle himself. "Why would you do such a thing? No, Viv will pay you. This is a gift from her."

Sam, who was nearly thirty-eight years of age, was no spring chicken. And to the fellowship, who believed young marriages are the best way to honor God, he was an old bachelor without much worth. He had seen the way Viv had looked at him when she had walked into the room, and how she had continued to make eye contact with him throughout dinner. Receiving her cues loud and clear, the man was not going to waste time. "This might seem premature, but since we are all here together, I'd like to ask permission to speak with you about something that matters very much to me."

GiGi was quick to give the clueless chump the floor.

"I have been watching you, Viv, for many weeks as you've come to fellowship with your sister and her family. I've seen the way you have grown in the ways of Yahweh, how you seek to honor Him. Just tonight, I am astounded by your beauty and grace. You are radiant in every way. So I would like to ask you and your parents for permission to begin courting you. Right away. My coming over here to finish the wood floors would be a way for us to see each other in a supervised way and would give me the chance to know the whole family at the same time. We aren't getting any younger, so I don't believe we have time to waste. If I'm being impetuous or too forward, please forgive me. But I'm acting from my heart's greatest desire. What do you say?"

GiGi was the first to speak, granting permission immediately. Poppy, following her lead, reluctantly nodded his head and also offered his approval. Now Viv's turn, she stopped to consider what she must do. On the one hand, going along with this ridiculous plan was intended for the good of her family. On the other, however, Sam was a real man with real feelings. He had just poured out his heart for her in front of her parents, which generated a strange, unexpected pang of guilt. Her hesitation proved to be too long for Sam. Standing to his feet, he made his way over to

Viv and took a knee by her side.

"Viv," he began, "I am not worthy of you. Don't you think I see that?" He then dropped his head, mocking himself with a laugh. "You have an education and a career while I sand and finish wood floors. I pretend to be a business owner, but I know the truth. I am no more than a blue-collar worker who happens to have a skill." Sam looked up, catching Viv's eyes. "You are such a rare find. From the moment I saw you at the first Sabbath service and heard your voice, I think I knew I would love you, and only you, Viv. And look at your family here, they are a real family. I've never had one of those, and it would be a true honor to call them my own."

GiGi piped in. "You may be jumping the gun on that, Sam."

"Oh, I know," he replied, "but sometimes it just feels good to dream. Do you know what I mean, ma'am?"

Viv had dated more men than she could shake a stick at and had fallen head over heels for most all of them. Around town, she was known as the woman who was in love with love. Something about this felt different to her, though. This man was for real. He didn't meet her qualifications at all, that was a glaring fact, but he was sincere and vulnerable. His left hand lay on the table before her. He still knelt on one knee, now looking in the direction of her mother. Taking his hand in hers, she was prepared to give an answer.

"Sam Smith," she said nervously, "it would make me the happiest girl in the county to court you." And to her own bewilderment, she almost meant it. If he hadn't been sporting that straggly beard that likely held as many germs as a toilet seat, she probably would have meant it. This guy was the exact opposite of any man she had ever dated, because he actually dared to try to sweep her off of her feet. To woo her. Sure, he was awkward, country, and a bit redneck, but he was also honorable and genuine. And more than anything else, he had called her a "rare find." What woman wouldn't want to be appreciated in that way? Viv decided in that moment that she would allow this strange man to adore her…to worship her…all for the sake of Mary.

His head snapped around to Viv at lightning-fast speed. If it hadn't been connected to his shoulders, it might have popped right off. His enthusiasm was palpable and warmed Viv's heart. She couldn't recall a time when someone was excited about her, not like this man was.

"Then it is official." His eyes, now filled with hope, gleamed. "If it's acceptable to everyone, I will begin refinishing the wood floors tomorrow afternoon, taking it one room at a time. And Viv, I would very much like to ask for time with you on the sun porch each evening, so we can get to know each other better."

GiGi's trap was set. Her plan was in action. Sam Smith and Viv would be instrumental in getting on the inside, to keep an eye on things at the fellowship until the spring could be sprung. As she turned in for the night, she thought of how proud she was of Viv.

Hadn't her daughter put on a believable act? Hadn't she thrown caution to the wind and fully embraced this character role? Sam was an old chump-dog in the scheme, but weren't we all pawns in someone's scheme? Even the government schemed to take our tax money in order to keep their voting block happy…and what about God? Didn't He create both good and evil as a way to scheme His way into our hearts? Hadn't He raised up and then hardened the heart of Pharaoh in order to promote His own glory? Arranged for Joseph to be sold into slavery? For the whale to swallow Jonah? And for Satan to tempt Job? Yes, if it was OK for God to scheme, then it was certainly OK for her.

That night, the matriarch of the family slept like a baby.

Chapter 14

The next few weeks flew by. Mary stuck by her convictions, having little to no contact with her parents, while Viv continued to court Sam, the wood floor guy. Believing Viv was still following the plan, GiGi didn't have a worry in the world. She had put all of her eggs into one basket, and she believed it would prove to be the wisest move she had ever made. Having a type A personality, Viv had honestly always been tough for GiGi to manage; in fact, in the past, if she had been asked to choose a favorite child, she would have picked Mary simply because Mary put up with her. But on this plan to bust Mary's family out of the cult, she and Viv had found common ground, unity. Two type A personalities working together made a powerful combo. Now, possibly for the first time since she was a little girl, Viv had won her mother's heart.

GiGi was wrong, of course. The enemy, who comes to steal, kill, and destroy, cannot be outmaneuvered by a human, even one as calculating as GiGi. Being a student of the human race since the beginning of time, he knew Viv's greatest desire was to be truly loved, and also knew Sam's daily prayer was to find a wife and to have a family. Putting the two of them together went as easy as joining mashed potatoes with gravy. The two, who were on their way to becoming lovebirds, thought the stars had aligned for them, but it was the dark one who had knitted them together, using their greatest desires against them as he often does. If he had his way, there would be more than one wedding on the horizon. GiGi was in for the shock of her life.

Emma was walking through the grocery with her mother when the opportunity presented itself. It was rare that the two were together without all of her other siblings, and on this particular day, her mom was stealing the time to ask her lots of questions about life in general. They had covered the topic of Wills, courtship, and had touched on the subject of marriage…and as the conversation waned, Emma decided to bring up the subject of her father and what she had heard when she was in the attic.

"Mom, would scripture prevent you from being able to keep a secret from dad?" she asked, as they searched for an organic brand of ketchup.

Her mother, curious, pretended to read the ingredients on a label. "That depends, sweetheart. I can't keep a secret from your dad if the subject has something to do with our family, because that wouldn't be fair to him. However, if a friend entrusts information to me that has nothing to do with our family, then yes, I believe scripture supports my keeping that information private." Placing the bottle back on the shelf and choosing another, she added: "Why do you ask?"

Emma got the answer she was looking for; it was also the answer she expected. Even if her mother wanted to keep the secret, her beliefs wouldn't allow it. For her, to keep a secret about her own husband would be to choose to sin against God. "Well, earlier we were talking about marriage, and I was just wondering about the rules of keeping secrets from Wills. That's all."

She hated lying to her mom, but under the circumstances, she didn't feel she had a choice. Her mother instinctively felt there was more to the story, but decided not to push the subject further. "Honey," she replied, "I want you to know you can always trust your dad and me with anything. You know that, don't you?"

In an effort to pacify, Emma shook her head, affirming that she knew what her mother was saying was true. In her heart, she wished it was. Knowing her dad and Scott were plotting to somehow take advantage of Wills's family kept her unsettled and even frightened her. This would be the last time Emma would try to confide in her mother about the matter.

Chapter 15

Dream Tide was the code name—the final piece of Brian and Scott's complex puzzle. Sold as new encryption technology that would change the face of piracy in the entertainment industry, the partners knew their ragtag fellowship members would never know it was a facade. A money-making scheme.

A private meeting was called out on the farm, a potluck dinner, in fact, to make sure everyone showed up. No true Southerner passes up a miscellany of food. After eating on the grounds, they were all called into the barn where chairs had been set up for the adults while children were encouraged to continue to play outside. With Brian seated in the front row, Scott, with a microphone in hand, began to speak.

"We've gathered here today because it is too dangerous to meet in our plaza anymore. The targeted attacks many of us have experienced have been not only vicious, but also unsettling. While we know Yahweh is in control, and this is all part of His plan, we must take this as a warning and begin to plan for our future.

"Brian and I purchased this farmland years ago, when we first felt the Father telling us that end times were drawing near. As you know, we've built three water towers and plan to build one or two more, which will prove to provide water when times get tough. And they will get a lot harder very soon since the signs of the times are everywhere, now, even in our own hometown…a place where we all believed we were safe.

"We have goats to provide milk, chickens to provide eggs, cattle to provide beef, a fully stocked pond to provide fish, and a huge vegetable garden…not to mention," he bragged, "in the last several years, we have become expert marksman. Just ask the deer, am I right?" He laughed and paused. "Oh yeah, we can't ask them, because we've killed every deer we've seen." The group laughed, considering how they had all become hunters. Each family had freezers full of deer meat and had taken great pride in their kills.

"I don't have to sell you; you all know what we have here. It's been a labor of love for us and has been the hardest thing we've ever set out to do. But we are committed to getting off the grid, to be a self-sustaining people, depending solely upon ourselves."

There it was, in a nutshell. Feeding the base desire in all men to take care of their family would get their attention, and the women would go right along. Scott and Brian had done one whale of a job getting the men to rise up while pushing their wives into submission.

"Our goal is to be the place of refuge when the tribulation comes. The false teaching of a pretribulation rapture is going to leave millions behind seeking a place that is safe. If those people are willing to put down their foolish doctrine to embrace the ways of Yahweh as we have, we will allow them in…then they, too, can find true salvation."

The crowd clapped eagerly with a bolt of energy that electrified the room.

"What they've bought into is a false religion." Shouts of "Amen" rang out randomly throughout the barn.

"Many of us have family members who have been lead to believe the lie. They think they are going to be whisked away in some big rapture even though scripture never mentions such a thing. What it does say is the end times will be like the days of Noah, and I ask you...did Yahweh rapture Noah and his family from the flood?" Scott broke his cadence for effect and then shouted a resounding: "*No!* He told them to build a boat so they could weather the forty-day storm!"

By this time, the gathering was getting whipped up into a near frenzy.

"When the death angel came, did Yahweh rapture the Hebrew people out of Egypt? *No!* He told them to put blood on their doorposts so their offspring could survive the great and terrible massacre."

The fellowship not only hung on every word Scott spoke, but they agreed with him wholeheartedly. To them, every other religion and faith on earth was mistaken and it was them, the chosen few, who held the truth. And it would be them, when the church as a whole was left baffled and bewildered during the Great Tribulation, forced to accept their theology had been false, who would lead them all in

Yahweh's ways. They would be like Noah, the seed of a new generation…like Moses, the forerunner of a new generation.

"But that's not all. In times of great change, Yahweh has always provided a plan for His people. They lacked nothing. Think about Joseph, thrown in a pit by his brothers and left for dead, sold into slavery, and then put into prison. But he became a great leader. Did Yahweh not then turn everything around and use Joseph to save all of the people when the famine came? Was grain not stored for the people just as we are storing up now, in this place, to care for our families?"

Scott was persuasive: a gifted orator. Brian was in on the plan but couldn't help but think of how believable the man standing before them all was.

"And that is where Dream Tide comes in." His voice broke as he pulled the microphone away from his mouth, clearly emotional. Taking a few seconds to gather himself for full dramatic effect, he continued, "Several months ago, Brian and I received a phone call from a Jewish man in Israel. One of our brothers who appreciates how, even though we are not of Jewish heritage, we are trying our best to follow the Torah. This Israeli just so happens to be a part of a multimillion-dollar corporation that has its hands in many pots, and one of them is technology. According to this man, Yahweh Himself spoke to this man in a dream and told Him to give a new piece of technology to us. He told Him we are the chosen ones who will be responsible for bringing the two branches together. Does Ezekiel chapter thirty-seven not prophesy that one stick will stand for Judah and the other for the lost tribes of Israel?"

The crowd, as one, shouted a resounding: "Yes!"

"And that those two branches will be joined to each other, made into one stick, by the hand of Yahweh?"

Again, a resounding "Yes!" rang through the wide-open room.

"And that Yahweh will be our God and that we will again be His people?"

The people stood, shouting praises to the Father as Scott looked on. Part of him felt a smidgen of sympathy for them, especially since the majority had been gathered into his flock from a place of brokenness, either because of a split in a church, a family disagreement, or some type of ongoing illness or disability. Scott and Brian had learned early on that the easiest fish to catch was the hungriest one. So, patiently they crafted their sport of becoming fishers of men by taking advantage of those who were "hungry" for emotional support. Sometimes, as in the case of Mary and Philip, it was by sheer good luck…but other times, they took time to search for these people. They had become quite good at it. The crowd settled, so he went on.

"In this man's dream, Yahweh told him we are the stick of Ephraim. We are part of the actual lost tribe of Israel, the set-apart ones. I have always believed it, and now it has been confirmed by a witness."

Every person stood, hands raised toward the sky, shouting, "Hallelujah!" Scott was now feeding into their pride and they were eating it up, as he knew they would.

"That's right! Praise Him! For He has found us worthy of such a calling. But listen; this is not all. He has provided for us lavishly and abundantly with this new technology called Dream Tide. It is an encryption technology that will be utilized by the entire entertainment industry to put a stop to piracy. And it is being gifted to us. We only need to come up with one hundred families who will each give a thousand dollars. That is the seed required of you to sow into this gift from God. And it is such a small amount of money when we consider the potential reward. If this is accepted by the entertainment industry, the one hundred partners, each owning a piece of this technology, could become millionaires. That is how big our Father is. We give and it is given back to us, pressed down, shaken together, and running over!"

Scott couldn't contain the group any longer. They were now hugging one another in complete celebration. Before the night ended, Scott knew he would hold $100,000 in his possession. These people would give, because they believed by giving, more was coming to them. Religious pride and greed fueled them, but faith in their unseen God would write his name on the checks.

Mary, Philip, Viv, and her new friend, Sam Smith, were at the meeting, in the front row. Philip, a very wealthy businessman, who had made his money with much hard work, was not one to part with it on a whim of emotion. But Mary, clinging to her hope for a miracle, persuaded him to write the check. Still plagued with guilt over his brief affair with Bonnie Cutless, he complied. As for Viv and Sam, since they were not married, each wrote a separate check. They were all in.

Chapter 16

GiGi and Poppy, keeping up with all the latest happenings through Viv, were now getting more and more concerned. The glint in Viv's eyes every time Sam's name was mentioned was not lost on either of them. Before long, if something drastic didn't happen, Viv would be hitched to Scott, and Wills would be tied down to Emma. Both, then, would be raising their families in some type of exclusionary cult system that impersonated Judaism.

Everyone who was fairly familiar with Philip, knew he could be extremely frugal, so when Viv brought news about how Scott and Brian had talked him into becoming the primary lender for all the members who wanted to own a part of the farmland commune and the mysterious business venture known as Dream Tide, they were beyond shocked. As it was, every day seemed to bear more bad news, and all they could do was stand by watching their family drift further into legalism. Their hands were tied, and even worse, Mary's family barely spoke to them anymore. Both often talked about how they wished they could go back to when they were pretending to be caught up in the cult, but it was too late for that now. They had taken their stand and there was no going back.

"Viv, are you still on our side?" GiGi asked one day on the phone, hoping her daughter would at least vacillate on the subject. "Or are you leaning more toward the Lost Tribe Fellowship and Sam Smith now?" Not one for beating around the bush, her question was out on the table and up for discussion.

In Viv's head, she probably knew this group was a cult. She was sensible, after all, and had been a skeptic from the beginning. All the men had those creepy long beards and wore *tzitzit* while the women adorned themselves with long hair and even longer skirts. At one point it had seemed grotesque to her, but now, as much as she hated to admit it, she sort of felt a part of something. A sensation of belonging was filling that empty hole in her heart, and she liked it. It didn't hurt, of course, that Sam had not tried to hide that he was head over heels for her. No man had ever treated with her with such honor and respect.

She collected her thoughts and prepared to answer, not wanting to give reason for alarm, but also wanting to be somewhat honest. "I'm not on anyone's side, Mom," Viv finally answered softly. The reply told GiGi all she already knew. Viv was being sucked in to Satan's voodoo.

"Of course you're not," the bird shot back with a chuckle. "I was silly to ask."

Preacher Walker and Jeannie had been meeting with Poppy and GiGi every week to pray for the family. They all longed for the day when they could worship together again in the old sanctuary where Mary had grown up. The pastor had told them he believed God was in control and would take care of all of it, that they only needed to continue to pray, wait and trust Him, but GiGi thought he was crazy. Waiting was not her game.

It was only because she had run out of ideas that she finally settled down. Frankly, all bottled up inside of her very put together outward appearance, there was a maniacal abductor who dreamed of hijacking her family and whisking them away to an obscure location where she could beat some sense into them. So much had changed; life would never be the same. GiGi was sure of it. When she heard news that Scott and Brian had never shown up for the Lost Tribe Fellowship camp meeting, understandably, the old bird nearly hyperventilated. Her whole neighborhood must have thought she had finally lost it when they saw her riding around with windows down, shouting, "Hallelujah! The chains of sin are being broken and my family is coming back to Jesus!" She drove around and around, shouting the same thing over and over again while tooting her car's horn. Perhaps she did go a little nuts that day, but who could really blame her?

The so-called camp meeting was to be a celebration, where each new owner of a plot of the farmland and shares of Dream Tide were to be given official certificates, declaring their proprietary rights. After waiting for more than an hour on the two hucksters and getting no response from their cell phones, the crowd had broken into a frenzy of worry. The police, convinced by the fellowship that the Jew haters who had been vandalizing all of their property had kidnapped Scott and Brian, put out a missing persons bulletin. It took several days before the truth began to finally dawn on them. The two had taken all the money and had left their families behind. The gaping chasm left in the hearts of the Lost Tribe Fellowship was more than most should be called to bear. They had been duped by two people they trusted most.

One might think an unholy mess like this would divide the fellowship of believers, but instead, for many, it drew them closer than ever. In all actuality, the scandal gave them new purpose. Not only did they have that one wretched incident in common, but what kept them forging forward more than anything else was their desire to care for Scott's and Brian's families, who had been left behind. How does a child process that his or her father was not who he pretended to be? That their whole lives were cooked up as a money-making scheme? Neither man had even taken the time to leave a note. Truly, they did not care.

The Tennessee Bureau of Investigation had assured the fellowship they would do everything they could to find the men and bring them to justice, but it would never happen. Their scheme was fail-safe. Because the crooks had been missing for several days before a crime was even suggested, the men had time to go and be anywhere. Scott and Brian's wives, eager to make things right with members of the fellowship, had offered the farm to all who had believed they were paying for actual plots, but no one took them up on their generous offer. The women had lost too much. They would now need to sell the farm to survive. As for Dream Tide, it ended up being a complete farce. A hoax. Each member of the makeshift church promised to pay Philip back every penny that had exchanged hands on their behalf, and while he appreciated their offer and knew their sentiments were genuine, he also knew the majority would never be able to afford it. That money, nearly all of his savings, was gone forever.

The story made the local news, but never reached national attention. Stories of the occult are not thought of as newsworthy unless people get killed as they did in the Jim Jones and Waco atrocities. The local attention, however, made running about town awkward for anyone who had been connected with the Lost Tribe Fellowship. Long skirts were seldom seen in Cleveland following the debacle, for fear one would be associated with the cult. Because Philip and Mary had funded the scoundrels, their names were plastered across social media daily. Once pillars in the community, they were now a laughingstock. As if the Bonnie Cutless affair hadn't been enough.

When the enemy comes to steal, kill, and destroy, he means business. And his favorite attack is against those who are sold out for God. How easy is it to be a Christian when things in life are easy? Praising God in the good times doesn't really amount to much of an offering of praise at all. And the enemy knows that. Seeing a kink in the Montgomerys' spiritual armor, he had pounced like a lion and had gone straight for the jugular. Fully aware of Mary's preoccupation with her special-needs daughter and a teenage son who was busy dipping his toe into the waters of rebellion, he had slithered in to place an attractive, very needy Bonnie Cutless in Philip's path. It is one of the oldest tricks in the book. No man ever climbs a tree to flee from an enticing woman. No man. Bonnie, blond and beautiful, had thrown herself at Philip, and over time, he succumbed.

Mary, in response, had filed for divorce.

Since God declares in scripture that He is the One who makes human beings deaf and mute, and the One who gives sight or makes a person blind, it was not the enemy who caused Miss Charity's heart to stop just prior to Thanksgiving. No, he doesn't hold that kind of power. But that lucky break did come at a perfect time for the enemy. The timing, though, couldn't have been worse for Philip and Mary. Already beaten up and battered, hanging on to the final vestiges of the little that was left of their frayed piece of rope, this blow caused them to let go of all hope and fall into what felt like a pit of nothingness.

What the two couldn't know was how Satan had requested permission to tempt them…to push them beyond their human limits…to see if they would rely on faith or if they would ultimately turn their backs on the One they proclaimed as God. Philip and Mary had exhibited moments of both strength and weakness. Mostly weakness. Never alone, however, God had sent His angels to watch over them. The enemy was at work, but he was on a leash. God's leash.

This latest soap opera drama with Scott and Brian was too much for Mary. To save face, she refused to let anyone know her true feelings, but God knew. If she had hated Him before, the woman now loathed Him. The thought of God being a father brought such anger to Mary's heart she could barely contain it. He wasn't a father at all. He was as big a fake as the two who had absconded with her family's money. Had she not stood in the face of each attack and cried out to God? Had she not acted in faith by embracing her Hebrew roots? Taken Philip back as her husband? Forsaken her parents in order to keep the Sabbath day and celebrate the holy days? The thought of all she had adjusted in her life in order to please the Almighty, with the hope of a miracle, made her want to throw her Bible in a blazing fire and watch it burn. It was now meaningless. Worthless. Words on a page meant to control the mindless sheep of the world. And she now clearly saw herself as a mindless sheep.

Mary had given up Christmas, Easter, pork, and shellfish. Her skirts were now long, her head covered, and her makeup minimal. She had ridded her home of television and computers in order to keep "the world" out, but God did not seem to care. Why? Because He was a made-up folk tale. And now she and Philip had given nearly every penny they had ever saved for the good of the fellowship, believing wholeheartedly that they were all in danger from a group of anti-Semites bent on hurting them. And it was all her fault for believing in a lie. Mary was finally ready to face facts. There would never be a miracle for Miss Charity.

Chapter 17

"Wills, I have to tell you something very important."
Emma managed to steal her mother's cell phone in the
middle of the night. Within the hour, her betrothed was
standing in her backyard, waiting for her to meet him.

They both knew a meeting like this was against the
fellowship's rules, but knowing Emma's grief over her
father, Wills was willing to do almost anything to help
bring healing to the situation. Upon seeing him, Emma ran
effortlessly through the long wispy grass, throwing her
arms with abandon around his neck. This was breaking a
major rule, too, since they were only allowed side hugs
until marriage. But he held her, allowing her to be the first
to pull away. And when Emma did push back, she looked
directly into Wills's eyes and kissed him. He didn't resist;
in fact, his heart pounded so loud he was certain she could
hear it. Emma wore no makeup, and her hair was hanging
in juvenile braids around her face, but to her suitor, she
looked as gorgeous as any female he had ever laid eyes on.
And here they were, alone for the first time, in the middle
of the night. It was all surreal.

Emma took his hand in hers and pulled him to a fallen tree
that had been fashioned into a bench by her dad and Scott
when she was just a little girl. She had sat in this exact spot
many times as her family roasted marshmallows over an
open bonfire. How could treasured memories turn so fast?
It had never crossed her mind that her dad would leave
them. While she hadn't always agreed with how harsh he

could sometimes be with the family, she always thought he loved them and that his intentions were noble. The two sat holding hands. Wills had no idea what was coming next, so he simply waited for her next move.

Emma breathed a deep sigh, dropped her head, and began, "I'm going to have to end our engagement, Wills." She then pulled off the small quarter-carat diamond ring he'd proudly purchased with his own money, placed it in the hand she'd been holding, and closed it tightly around the ring. "My dad obviously arranged our relationship so he could get his hands into your daddy's deep pockets," she mocked, her Southern accent laced with a redneck harshness, "and as much as my mom would probably like to pawn me off to someone as nice as you, she's going to need me to get a job and help financially take care of my little brothers and sisters. The new baby is due soon, so there is no possible way she can go to work."

In all the chaos, Wills hadn't even considered the unborn child Brian had left behind. He certainly didn't know what to say since this was all unexpected. Her father's actions, though not Emma's fault, had rocked him to the core, too. There was even a small part of him that believed Emma's mother might have been a party to the crime. How could two men carry on a bait-and-switch for that many years? And without their wives having a clue? If he ever were to find out that was the case, he knew he could never feel right about marrying into a family that had knowingly taken so much from his own family. Betraying his own uneasy feelings about what the future held for them, though, the last thing he wanted Emma to see in him was weakness. Right now, above all else, she deserved integrity, strength, honor, and loyalty.

"Emma—" he began.

"No, Wills," she interrupted sharply, "don't say anything. If you really care about me, you will just listen and give me whatever I ask of you."

Emma had never told another soul about the conversation she'd heard that day in the attic between her father and Scott, but under the moonlight, sitting on an old beloved log, she told him everything. She also admitted she was questioning everything she thought she knew about God and was now even unsure whether she would ever marry after what her father had done to them all. Emma asked him to let her go.

Honoring her wishes, Wills listened intently, saying nothing. He hung on every word, accepting that this moment would indeed usher in the end of their courtship. She was correct about many things, but one thing in particular. No matter how unfair it seemed, Emma would have to go to work to help care for her family, at least until her mother could sell the farm. Her dad had left behind a horde of kids to feed, clothe, teach, and care for. What was the man thinking? Did he and Scott decide a great number of children would make their cult fiction more believable? Were they that deranged? Whatever the reason, it left their families in dire straits.

Throwing caution to the wind, Emma and Wills allowed their forbidden kisses to be a sweet good-bye. When the young girl finally stood to leave, she bent down to take Wills's face in her hands and whispered, "I am so sorry for what my dad did to your family. If it were in my power, I would change it all just so I could be with you." Then she was gone.

Managing to turn back toward the house before tears filled her eyes, Emma left knowing she had done Wills a huge favor. Wasn't he the one with the heart of a golden retriever? Yes, he surely would have gone through with the wedding even if only to make her happy; loyalty was both his greatest attribute and weakness. Although something inside Emma's heart told her she had most likely let her soul mate go, because she loved Wills Montgomery with the purest of hearts, she earnestly wanted him to find someone who wouldn't be a constant reminder of the humiliation that had been brought upon his family.

The news of the broken courtship spread like a wild fire through the fellowship. Wills hoped no one would get involved, but they all did. Phone calls were made to Philip and Mary, who quickly revealed they had been as surprised as anyone else. Desperate to keep their group together, any division, even one between two as young as Wills and Emma, had to be managed with the greatest of care.

"I don't care what the cult says." GiGi's bite was more aggressive than usual. The old bird had turned pure pit bull. "This break-up is the best thing for everyone."

Mary was sick of her life and everyone in it save her children, so on this point, she agreed with her momma. "You are singing to the choir. Do you really think I want my son to marry into the family that stole our life savings?" The two were meeting for a quick lunch at Jenkins to discuss the latest happenings with Viv, but Mary found herself in a mood to let her mom in on a few secrets. "If I wanted to divorce Philip, thanks to Cruel and Crueler, that would now be a financial impossibility. I am trapped."

"Divorce Philip?" GiGi cried. "Are you serious, Mary? You two seem to me to be as happy as ever." She was curious and was willing to dig as deep as Mary would allow, but she would not be pushy. Not yet. This would mark the first time her daughter had wanted to chat with her in a long time, and she would not mess things up.

"Listen, Mom, I'm going to level with you." Mary's eyes bore into her mother's. "I am finally willing to admit that you and Daddy were right. I have dragged my family into a cult." Hearing the words spoken aloud infuriated Mary. How could she have been such a fool? "And now we have to save Viv."

GiGi's eyes bugged clear out of her head as her bright-red lips pursed tight like a pocketbook. She hadn't planned for this at all. In fact, she had planned to greet Mary with pure acceptance of the cult...with sorrow for Wills's failed courtship...with tears if need be. The woman had prepared to lie like a dying dog. But this? Her daughter seeing the truth? "Oh Lordy! Butter my biscuit and slather me on like fresh peach preserves! God is finally answering all of my prayers." In the excitement of the moment, it dawned on her that she might have offended her daughter with the word *God*. "I meant to say, Yahweh has answered my prayers. Sorry about that slip-up, honey."

Mary rolled her eyes and couldn't help but smile. "Look, I don't care what you call Him…God, Jesus, Yahweh, Yeshua, Muhammad, Buddha…I am stepping away from all that. At least for now."

Reaching across the table, GiGi touched Mary's hand. Still as beautiful as ever, Mary did look tired.

"Well, sugar, after all you have been through, I think God would understand your need for a little space and time. I did notice you weren't wearing the long Amish skirt or the little doily on your head, but I was afraid to hope." She grinned, allowing her eyes to twinkle, just so Mary would buy into her syrupy sweet seduction, but then quickly excused herself from the table to find an empty bathroom stall. She sat, fully clothed, upon the white throne and sent a text message to someone who needed a piece of her mind—Preacher Walker.

It read: *I don't know how hard you've been praying, but it's obviously not hard enough. You've been saying we're supposed to wait and let God take care of this mess, and now Mary is taking a break from God. Is that good? No, I don't think so! It's time for a new plan. Prayer is not cutting it.*

When she returned to the table, their food was waiting. Mary felt happy to be with her mother again; she hadn't realized how much she'd missed her. "Now, Mom, let's talk about how we're going to keep Viv from making the biggest mistake of her life."

GiGi took her napkin and placed it into her lap. Normally she would have prayed over the food, but not today. The bird was not about to rock that boat. She and Mary were a team again.

Chapter 18

Because the family had been through so much in a short period of time, every member was in self-preservation mode, meaning they were incapable of looking out for one another. And this, for the record, is how the enemy prefers things to be in any family. Tate and Miss Charity were the only two who had escaped the melodrama. Tate was too young to fully comprehend what was happening, and Miss Charity, well, she was protected from such things. Everyone else, however, was under the thumb of extreme pressure.

Philip, a local business owner, was finding people in Cleveland were more than reluctant to do business with someone who had dabbled in the occult. His business had somehow survived the affair with Bonnie, which was a miracle given the small Christian town frowned upon such things, but he feared this latest situation might take him down. Most of his days were now spent in the office doing damage control, calling on clients, attempting to put their minds at ease. Several of his key employees had already left, putting the day-to-day work routine at risk. Hiring was difficult, too. The only people willing to take a job from him were members of his fellowship, and hiring them would only perpetuate his mounting problems. The life Philip had worked so hard to build for his family was crumbling, and there was nothing he could do about it.

Having given up football to follow what he believed was the Father's will in his life, Wills was now homeschooled and had been forsaken by all of his lifelong friends, who now considered him strange. When out in town, he noticed his peers turning in the opposite direction to avoid contact with him. Once popular, Wills was now ostracized, and the realization that he had given up everything for Emma and the Lost Tribe Fellowship weighed heavy on him. He felt like a complete fool, a clown. He had given up the chance of a football scholarship, and now that his family had lost a chunk of their savings, he would never go to college. Depression began to wrap its ugly claws around his brain, and thoughts of running away, finding a drug to dull the pain, or committing suicide ravaged his thoughts. Most nights he didn't sleep. Still a teenage boy, Wills was unable to process the turmoil without the help of his parents, and they were too busy trying to survive to notice.

Wanting desperately to get married, Viv questioned whether Sam might move on from her like every other man had in the past. Did she love him? Not especially, but maybe a little. She did know if she could drag him down the aisle, he would love her unconditionally for life and would be a dutiful husband. Possibly not the most romantic scenario, but at her age, could she really be picky? The bachelorette had even cooked up a foolproof plan of her own until Brian and Scott did their little number. Once married, she had planned to go back to her normal style of fashion and to return to Preacher Walker's church for the Sunday morning services. While she guessed it would make Sam very unhappy, she knew he wouldn't leave her over it. Divorce for Sam would be out of the question…against the core of his beliefs. Viv had found a way to make her dreams come true. An owner of his own business, be it only a wood floor business, Sam did earn good money, so with their combined salaries, they could afford a nice home. And both wanted children, which was the true impetus behind her moment of madness. But now, with the latest catastrophe, everything was subject to change, and it was fast becoming a heavy burden for Viv to carry. She had always thought it beneath her to trap a man into marriage, but her ever-waking thought was on just that.

GiGi and Poppy were, of course, worried sick over their family. And Mary was as bitter as ever, a ticking time bomb, though she still hid it fairly well. Each family member carried his or her own burdens, obsessing over them, nurturing them, feeding them, and thus allowing them to grow.

"I'm telling you," the pastor argued, "I believe the Lord Himself told me that we don't need to butt in on Mary's business. We are supposed to wait and pray."

GiGi had dragged Poppy over to Preacher Walker and Jeannie's house in a flurry of worry. Relentless, she was not going to give up. "I know you are a man of God and all, but I wonder if you haven't misinterpreted something here. Have you considered that?"

The pastor with the gentle soul could be no more and no less than what he was. Not seminary trained, his beliefs had been built upon worn-out knees that had submissively bent to seek truth from his Savior through prayer. The Word said to pray without ceasing, and the older gentleman had taken that literally. Never claiming to understand all the words written in the Bible, he always stood by what he felt to be Jesus's greatest command: love God and love people. Now seated in a chair across the room from two old friends, he placed his elbows on his knees and rubbed his hands together. His voice, soft and kind, matched the look in his eyes. "I've considered it every time you've questioned me," he answered. "But every single time, I just know in my spirit that we aren't supposed to interfere. I believe God wants us to wait."

"But what good can come from waiting? Things are just getting more and more messed up." GiGi, if given an answer she was looking for, might have been satisfied for a while. But the pastor could not guarantee that her family was going to come out on the other side of this debacle unscathed.

"I actually think a lot of good can come from waitin' on the Lord," he spoke in his familiar, folksy way, knowing his words were not going to be what she was wanting to hear. "He is the author of your family's story and is writing it just the way He pleases. If you try to fight him on it, you just aren't going to get anywhere." He gave a slight giggle. "You might end up makin' things worse." Sincerity dripped from the man who now sat grinning at the woman who was bent on taking him head-on.

"Things couldn't get any worse. Are you kidding?" GiGi fired back. "You know, maybe you're just too old-fashioned for the times. There once was a time when families stuck together no matter what, but not anymore. If I sit around and do nothing, I will lose them all."

Sitting back in his chair, the older gentleman rubbed his age-worn hands through his crown of silvery-white hair and chuckled again. Fear was driving GiGi, and he knew it. Fear is the driving force behind the bad decisions most people make. Instead of getting flabbergasted and arguing with her, he decided to remind her of a story. "Do you remember Abraham?"

"Abraham from the Bible?" GiGi did not come to the pastor's house for a sermon and was quick to remind him of that. "What on God's green earth does Abraham have to do with my Mary? He was an ancient old man with a long robe and Mary isn't. Please, for the love of my sanity, which is running very thin at this point, let's try to stay on the subject."

But he wasn't one to give up and pressed on. "I wasn't comparing that old ancient man to Mary...I was comparing him to you." He laughed out loud upon seeing the reaction his statement got from the old bird. If looks could kill, let's just say, Preacher Walker would have been dead on the spot. He continued, "Abraham was an old man when God told him he and his wife, Sarah, would have kids. He told them they would have so many descendants, in fact, that they would number the sand on the sea shore and the stars in the sky if they could be counted." He paused, reflecting on the absolute wonder of such an amazing Father who sees ahead and provides. He resumed his speech. "But Abraham and Sarah became impatient because they didn't want to wait on the Lord. And you know what? They had good reason to doubt God, since they were both gettin' on up in age. Both of 'em were way older than Jeannie and me."

"I know what happened." GiGi butted in. "I'm not a complete idiot when it comes to the Good Book. Abraham slept with one of the slaves, and she had his firstborn, Ishmael. But eventually Sarah did have Isaac, so it all worked out even though it would have made me mad as a hatter if Pops here had had 'whoop de doo' with some other woman under my nose."

The pastor allowed her to get in her two cents but then asked, "Well, that was the result, yes, but what was the consequence of Abraham and Sarah's choice to not wait on God?"

This time Poppy interjected. "We now have the Arabs versus the Jews. It's been constant conflict that has impacted our entire world."

The pastor gave a sad smile, picked up the worn Bible lying on the small wooden table at his side, and patted it hard. "The truest test of our faith is in how we wait."

Poppy and Jeannie tried their level best to help Preacher Walker convince GiGi as the evening progressed, but she would not bend. She was going to save her daughter come hell or high water, and this group was not going to stand in her way. Finally giving up, GiGi rose with full indignation, grabbed her purse, and marched toward the door. "Obviously I have come to the wrong church for help." She threw the barb, hoping it would sting.

Jeannie couldn't stand it. Yes, they had been friends for nearly a lifetime, but the woman was crossing some lines by being so haughty. "You know what?" she called out to GiGi with a tone that caused the old bird's head to snap around. "Maybe you have a bigger fish to fry right under your own nose."

"Now, Jeannie, don't say anything you might regret," the preacher said, half-hoping she'd give GiGi a good wallop instead of trying to argue with her.

Jeannie heard the warning but was not about to back down. "Maybe God is telling you to let the thing with Mary go because He is going to handle that situation while you need to focus on Viv!" she nearly shouted. "I'm telling you, Viv is going to marry that man with the long fuzzy beard and you're going to end up with an eighteen-passenger van full of grandsons who look just like him. And I will laugh every time I see them because you deserve it!"

Well, that was the limit. GiGi, appalled by what her longtime friend had said, opened the front door and slammed it hard behind her, leaving Poppy inside.

But indignation wasn't what was most present inside her mind any longer, for now she was plagued by the visualization of a bunch of little boys running amok sporting long grungy beards and *tzitzit*. She bristled at the thought. Poppy said his good-byes, apologized for his wife, and met her in the car.

"You were rude to our friends tonight and in their house." He fussed while starting his car. "That just isn't right. I know you are worried sick over our family, but I am ashamed of your behavior tonight." The car rumbled to a start, making an angry sputter to match that of the brewing man behind the wheel.

GiGi, in response, burst into tears. She bawled as he drove back to the house, crying so hard, she could barely catch a breath. Finally, Poppy decided she had suffered enough. "Listen," he suggested with the most calming tone he could manage, "if you will just call Preacher Walker and Jeannie to tell them you are sorry for how you acted, I'm sure they'll forgive and forget. They are the best people I know." He reached over and rubbed her shoulder as he drove.

Shoving his hand away with a quick jerk, GiGi shot back:

"What on earth are you gabbing about? I'm not one bit sorry for what I said, and I should be the best person you know since I've put up with you all these years." She had been crying, but obviously not from sorrow. "I will find a plan to bring Mary and the kids back to God if it kills me. And no matter what anybody says, prayer is just not working and this is completely different than the story of Abraham and Sarah. I'm telling you as sure as I'm sitting here in this car, God wants us to get off of our backsides and do something!"

"If you're not sorry about how you acted at Preacher and Jeannie's, then why all the crying?" he asked.

She took a deep breath and tried to hold back her tears, but they started coming again. The woman was wrought with emotion. "I'm thinking of how ugly our grandkids will be if Viv marries Sam Smith. Pops, we have to do something right away to break that up! Both of our daughters are flubbing up and making disasters out of their lives." Wiping the tears off of her face with an absentminded swipe of her hand, she added, "This is an embarrassment to me and should be to you, too. It's a reflection of our parenting skills." Letting out a deep breath, she started bawling again. "Somewhere along the line, we failed. We thought we were the best parents on the earth, but we were just big foolish fuddy-duddies the whole time. And now Viv's ugly little kids are going to be a reminder for the rest of our days."

He laughed out loud. It was one of those laughs that took

his own breath away, the kind that splits your sides and makes you hurt. "That's a prime example of what happens when you get busy meddling instead of staying on your knees praying. Remember, *you* are the reason Viv is with Sam! He was your secret weapon to get Viv into the Lost Tribe Fellowship's inner circle, and I will be reminding you of that every time one of those ugly bearded kids comes over to our house." He guffawed. "This one is on you, and you're not dragging me in on it."

GiGi cried even harder than before. She couldn't argue with her husband; Sam Smith had been her idea and she had pushed him on Viv with the veracity of a Mack truck. The truth slapped her silly, right across the barely wrinkled face that belied her true age. "Those little bearded grandbabies will be my burden to carry, Pops." Martyrdom took over as she spoke. "I won't put it on you at all. I'll take the full blame of it and love 'em regardless of how ugly the little ankle-biters are."

Back at Sam's place, Viv was gathering courage to implement her plans of seduction. How far would it go? She didn't know. But her goal was a marriage, a house, and a baby. That much she *did* know.

Chapter 19

To describe the enemy as sinister can be likened to characterizing a tree as something that is green. Yes, for the most part, trees are green, but do they not morph as a chameleon into brilliant hues of red, gold, and fiery orange just before the cold winter comes to ravage their leaves? Providing shade and shelter for all who seek it, do they not also produce fruits and nuts, and do they not provide oxygen, required for the sustenance of life, while simultaneously storing carbon dioxide? The wood from a tree can be fashioned into magnificent art, handcrafted for the enjoyment of the most royal of royalty…transformed into a simple cradle that will hold the weakest among us…or even hewn into ordinary planks to be walked upon by random passersby who will never notice them. To describe a tree as green would be to miss its full potential, just as to describe the enemy as sinister, would be to miss his, too.

Oftentimes, as believers in the One True God, we are guilty of slapping a preconceived label on the devil and his minions. Hearkening back to our childhood days in Sunday school class, we visualize him as one who is anti-God instead of one who masquerades as God. To get to God's people, wouldn't he necessarily have to enter by way of the church? Or else produce his own eerily similar version of church? Scripture encourages the followers to be humble as lambs but sly as foxes. How many who are in the church, wholeheartedly seeking the will of the Father, instead become prideful lambs who are brilliantly outfoxed, altogether missing the fact that the message has either been watered down or slightly altered?

When our version of "Who" God is becomes distorted, our life's foundation shifts. The stronger and more stable the foundation, the more difficult the damage will be. Those with the firmest foundations fall the hardest when the earthquake comes. The aftershock is messy, leaving behind millions of broken pieces that will never come back together as they once were.

As followers of the Way, many of us believe things to be a certain way, that if we follow preordained steps and participate in certain rituals, we will be the untouchables. Not to mention, we'll also go to heaven. And isn't that our goal? We wear badges of grace, but perhaps our lives bear more semblance to a legalistic soldier ordered to establish daily checkpoints:

Read the Bible...check.

Pray before meals...check.

Go to church...check.

Tithe...check.

Don't curse, or smoke, or become drunk, or scream at your children, or disobey your parents, or watch inappropriate television, or gossip (at least not in the presence of other believers).

Check, check, check, check, and check.

And this long list of checks, we assume, is our greatest strength, when in reality, it personifies our greatest weakness. The longer the list, then, the weaker we are. Why? Because it is a farce. It is anti-God.

Scripture says the Savior came to set the captives free, so anything that imprisons us has necessarily been established by the enemy. Yes, he is so much more than that green tree we see every day of our lives but never take note of. He isn't the antithesis of God at all. He is a slightly altered version of God who can visit you through the words of a pastor, a spouse, a friend, or a neighbor…he can be friendly and kind or haughty and hateful…beautiful or ugly…strong or weak. Whatever you need him to be, you can believe, he will be that.

Wills was sitting on his bed one evening. The house was quiet. Everyone else was in bed asleep.

Tapping at his door, Mary entered.

"I saw your light was still on," she said softly, scooting over to the bed in her slippers, preparing to sit down beside him. "I've been hoping we'd get some time together, just you and me." Placing her head on his shoulder, she ran her arm up through his. "How are you managing this break-up with Emma?"

"I'll be all right," he answered, covering the pain that had pulled the ground right out from beneath his feet. It had been his own earthquake, and as a result, his reality had broken into millions of pieces. Now dangling in midair, Wills pointed his toes as hard as he could, seeking the foundation he once knew. But it was gone.

What Mary didn't know was how Wills blamed himself for everything. The affair between Philip and Bonnie Cutless would have never happened had he not been friends with Bonnie's son, Crew. And now, his family had lost almost all of their savings. His father was facing losing the family business, and there was a strained relationship between his parents and grandparents and Preacher Walker and Jeannie. It was all because of him. He had made horrible decisions that had brought ruin on his family, and he despised himself for it.

Mary, concerned about her own despair way too much to notice the hurt behind her son's words, took her hand and tussled his hair with her fingers. His hair was still as soft as it was when he was a baby. Oh, how she loved him. "I have made so many mistakes, and if I'd been more on guard, you wouldn't have gotten hurt like this. This was my fault, Wills, and I hope you can forgive me." She took his right ear between her finger and thumb and rubbed it gently as a tear escaped from one of her eyes.

Wills felt confused. "What mistakes? Mom, you didn't do anything wrong."

Mary, facing Wills, crossed her legs, and slumped over,

allowing her elbows to rest on her knees. "I have made mistakes, too many to count. None of this was your fault. As your momma, I'm supposed to be aware and on guard, and I wasn't. With Miss Charity's heart issues, I put my guard down." Her words were heavy, but her voice soft and broken.

"I've made two gigantic mistakes," she continued. "My first was that I ever allowed myself to believe in God, because, let's face, it, if there really was a God, would He allow us to go through all of this crap?" She feigned a laugh. "And second, that I didn't go ahead and divorce your dad when he took off with Bonnie. Had I not bought into religion, I would be keeping my house and collecting a sizable child-support check every month." She snapped her fingers. "Easy come, easy go, right?"

Her words hung in the air, giving Wills that eerie feeling that things in his life were not going to work out this time.

"We're going to lose our house?" he gasped, honestly surprised by this new revelation.

His mother fell back on the bed, pulled a pillow up underneath her head, and huffed. "Well, your dad's business is now floundering, which means we will have a drastic cut in earnings, and our savings is all but depleted. So yes, we are probably going to have to sell this old house and move. It's just a house. Par for the course, right?"

"But this has been our home, like, forever." He could feel

his heart racing with panic. On top of all the other disasters he had caused, now Miss Charity would lose her home. Tate, it wouldn't affect so much, but for Miss Charity, their home represented safety and security.

When Mary left his room, Wills picked up his computer and searched: *How much vodka until you get drunk?*

Standing on a chair, he pushed the items on his top shelf to the side to reveal three full bottles of vodka that he'd taken from Crew's basement more than a year ago. He'd swiped them to keep his friend from drinking and had intended to pour it all down his sink. Not wanting his parents to catch him in the act, he had hidden it instead.

Wills pulled open a dresser drawer and, after rummaging through a pile of socks, spotted a small shot glass bearing the name of his favorite NFL football team, the Tennessee Titans. He had won it at a dirty Santa party a few years back, not even knowing, at that time, what a shot glass was. Taking it in hand, he opened the bottle.

Wills poured his first drink into the shot glass and drank it. It burned his throat, causing him to cough hard. But he poured another. And another. And another.

After several minutes, the young former quarterback who had forsaken his dreams for a girl no longer cared about his troubles.

Acknowledgments

This book was written for all who have fallen hard for a false religion with hope of a miracle. I am one of those people. Life's path is so difficult, friend. It is full of ups and downs, twists and turns…we fall into a pothole one day and stumble through a patch of poison ivy the next…but God sees and knows. One day, in light of eternity, it will all make perfect sense. I honestly believe that. Until then, though, we must press on. The way I see it, as long as we are moving forward, one step at a time and one day at a time, we will surely make it to the other side. Much love to you from a former Cult Keeper.

www.ingramcontent.com/pod-product-compliance
Lightning Source LLC
Chambersburg PA
CBHW070932130626
46555CB00001B/390